First Responder
THE RESCUE SQUAD

D0877434

First Responder
THE RESCUE SQUAD

Lock Boyce

FIRST RESPONDER THE RESCUE SQUAD

iUniverse books may be ordered through booksellers or by contacting:

iUniverse
1663 Liberty Drive
Bloomington, IN 47403
www.iuniverse.com
1-800-Authors (1-800-288-4677)

Because of the dynamic nature of the Internet, any web addresses or links contained in this book may have changed since publication and may no longer be valid. The views expressed in this work are solely those of the author and do not necessarily reflect the views of the publisher, and the publisher hereby disclaims any responsibility for them.

Any people depicted in stock imagery provided by Getty Images are models, and such images are being used for illustrative purposes only.
Certain stock imagery © Getty Images.

ISBN: 978-1-5320-8270-2 (sc)
ISBN: 978-1-5320-8271-9 (e)

Library of Congress Control Number: 2019915064

Print information available on the last page.

iUniverse rev. date: 09/13/2019

Dedicated to those, all those, past, present and future, who volunteer your time as a rescue squad member. God Bless you, you are on the side of the Angels.

Lock Boyce

"...to be there was to remember..."
Melanie

"If you want to tell the truth, write fiction..."
William Faulkner

CHAPTER ONE

1989

And then… and then… sometimes, your crazy, jealous, bitch of a girlfriend grabs the wheel and pushes down hard with her foot on top of your foot on top of the accelerator pedal and then, then she screams, "I'm gonna kill us all you motherfucker!" This last yahoo was interrupted by a deafening crash as the Monte Carlo hit the cement side of the Spoon Creek Bridge and Renee's crazy ass was flung through the windshield. At least that's what happened to the then boyfriend Mr. Randy McAllen one early gray September morning.

Now Mr. McAllen was a *Pagan,* not by religious conviction but by his affiliation with the Pagan's Motorcycle Club. The Pagans are "one-percenters." If ninety-nine percent of motorcyclists are law-abiding honest citizens, then the one-percenters are, well, not. Founded in 1959 in Maryland they once exclusively rode Triumph motorcycles but by 1989, they rode only Harleys, big Harleys: 900 c.c.'s or bigger. In fact, the ownership of such a machine is one of the requirements for membership. You must also be a heterosexual male, white, at least twenty- one years old and you must have committed a major crime. The Club was strongest in Virginia and North Carolina.

By 1989 the Pagans had become businessmen in a big business and that business was crime. They sold illegal drugs in many areas; they organized, and they controlled. Their stock and trade, their bread and butter, so to speak was methamphetamine the demand for which was immense in the South. They also sold firearms of all types as well as explosives. Oddly, they had allied themselves with the mafia in the southeastern United States and were known as the enforcers for the mob. It was no wonder that many law enforcement officials considered the Pagans more dangerous and violent than the Hell's Angels.

Randy McAllen had been a full patch member for fifteen years, he had just turned forty, but he could easily pass for sixty. He was compact, only five feet ten inches and about 175 pounds; his thin body was rock hard and there was no mistaking his physical strength. He gave the impression of a tightly coiled spring, ready to explode with stunning speed. He had the body of an athlete, a wrestler perhaps, or an adult chimpanzee. His face made him look older. It was weathered with deep lines etched into leathery brown skin. The eyes were black and quick, constantly in motion taking in all the information they could see. Like a hunter, he took nothing in his environment for granted. The bushy eyebrows like the other abundant hair on his head were mostly gray with only flecks of black to reminisce about the original color. There was a short but full beard and moustache. His hair was thick and long, usually a bit greasy. When Randy McAllen looked at a man, he always squinted both eyes and fixed the man in a chilling cold stare that communicated pure menace. That gaze was a threat and nothing less. Essentially all men were regarded as opponents to be intimidated. It was a habit he picked up in prison.

Randy's head was always covered with a hat, a dew-rag or a helmet. He was rarely seen not wearing his "cuts" or "cut offs." "Cuts" are blue jean jackets with the sleeves cut off. In warm weather, he would wear only his cuts and a pair of jeans with engineer boots. In cold weather he might wear a heavy leather jacket, but his cuts would be worn over it. On the back of the cuts was sewn the Pagan's patch or colors: big, red gothic letters spelling out *Pagan's* over an image of the Norse fire giant Surtr, squatting on the sun and holding his fire sword in his right hand. Surtr in Norse mythology was the guardian of fire. Dark and swarthy, he was supposed to come from the south with his flaming sword and engulf the world in fire. Not surprisingly, Surtr was also the god of chaos. Below the image of the skeletal figure were the letters *M.C.* for "Motorcycle Club." Missing on a Pagan emblem was any sort of geographical designation. The Hell's Angels have their chapter name included in their colors, but the Pagans don't freely offer information to anyone. In fact, most Pagans wear a tattoo: NUNYA meaning "None ya fucking business."

When Randy McAllen looked at a woman (which was often) his demeanor changed. His eyebrows lifted, the eyes softened, and he smiled with his clean white teeth and gold crowns. If he was attracted to a "type" it was loud women with large breasts and big round buttocks. Brains were not required. Randy McAllen's ideal woman might well have resembled Gaston Lochaises' famous statue, *Torso*, all tits and ass, no head, no hands, no feet. His current squeeze was Renee Kits. She liked to party. She liked to drink. She liked to ride motorcycles and she liked to fuck. Beyond that, she and Randy had little in common, but who cared? He supported her and if he wanted her, she was there, otherwise, she left him alone. He was looking for a woman, not a soul mate and the arrangement had worked for three years. They rarely argued but then they didn't talk that much either. She assumed there were other women in Randy's life, but he never threw it in her face or publicly disrespected her. For a Pagan, it passed for a committed relationship.

Renee lived in Randy's modest house in Martinsville. It was the house he grew up in. It had not been a happy childhood. His father worked as a truck driver for Tultex, a textile manufacturer. His mother worked for K-Mart. There were five children and there was never enough money. His daddy's hobby was drinking and beating the hell out of his family. Life was so miserable that Randy left home as soon as he could and found love. A love for motorcycles. He dropped out of high school but soon found out that lawful work for dropouts was scarce and low paid, so he turned to crime. Randy wasn't stupid but he was inexperienced, he went almost straight from high school to the first of many jails. He was serving time in Mecklenburg for felony sale and distribution of narcotics when he was recruited by the Pagans. They taught him how to commit the crime and not do the time. Before long, Randy started accumulating money. Serious money. He had become a businessman. He was very good at the business.

The Pagans may have been illicit businessmen, but they didn't have conventions. They had pig pickings. And so, in late September, Randy and Renee went to a pig picking on a farm near Hillsville. It was a four-day affair with almost three hundred members present. Usually Randy would have ridden his 1200 cc modified Harley Davidson Super Glide, but Renee was down with her back, so they drove her black '76 Monte Carlo two-door coupe.

Back in the sixties and early seventies, a gathering of Pagans would have been reported in the press as "an orgy of sex, drugs and violence." Times had changed. That kind of crap attracted unwanted attention. The average Pagan was older and wiser. They were dealers with something to lose. State Police cars and County cruisers patrolled the public roads around the farm with no legal right to come on the premises without good reason, and the Pagans made sure there was no good reason. There was lots of whiskey (Rebel Yell was preferred), beer and plenty of food (catered).

The best local bands provided the entertainment which had to be Southern Rock and loud. If you dared play *Free Bird* (the Pagan's unofficial anthem) you better be perfect.

The motorcycles were the central feature. Hundreds of them. Big, flashy machines as prized as any horse. The ground-shaking, deep roar of so many huge engines made certain that everyone knew the Pagans were here. Each of these mechanical horses carried a stoney faced driver, his lady clinging to his back and on his back was a cut with the Pagan's colors. It had the feel of some ancient rite; a gathering of the clans so to speak or perhaps a rendezvous of Mountain Men or even an Indian Pow Wow. As long as there have been men, men who were warriors, there have been such gatherings. In 1989, the Pagans Motorcycle Club members were such warriors, the dark knights, thundering out of the South bringing with them fire and the threat of chaos.

As at any meeting, business was conducted but not in large groups. Deals were made, information exchanged, and problems solved in small knots of men on the fringes. Two, three or four Pagans, talking quietly without looking directly at each other and sharing thoughts as much with small movements of the head and eyes as with words.

While conventional business leaders may lie, cheat and steal among themselves, the Pagans had a strict code of survival. You didn't lie to or steal from another Pagan, nor do you cheat your brothers. Above all, you keep the secrets of the club. A Pagan who violated the code would possibly wind up dead, rotting away in some remote place until all that remained was a skull with a bullet rattling around where the brain had once been. This code gave the Pagans a sense of superiority over a world they found filled with crooked cops, paid-off prosecutors and dirty judges. The Pagans thought of themselves as tougher, stronger, braver and more trustworthy than the "normal" society that surrounded them. If a Pagan told something to another Pagan or made a deal with another Pagan you could count on it. This trust meant that business would be conducted in small groups without a lot of witnesses, without written contracts and without lawyers. When you're in the business the Pagans were in, there were real advantages to such a system.

It was before the Spoon Creek Bridge smasheroo that Randy McAllen came into the possession of a small zip-lock bag filled with crystal meth from a new supplier. He got the sample from a huge Pagan with a flowing gray beard known as "Blade". It was a promise of more to come. Randy stuck the sample in the pocket of his cuts. He wanted to be able to lose it quickly if need be. Possession of that much meth and the .45 automatic in his belt by a convicted felon like Randy could easily lead to what would be essentially a life sentence in the Virginia Department of Corrections.

The gathering was not all work. The nights consisted of telling stories, laughing, drinking, eating, listening to the music and enjoying the company of women. There were a lot of women. Biker chicks. Those who came with and stayed with a man, known as "ladies" and those who came by themselves and were looking for a Pagan of their own. These were referred to as "strays" and one of these "strays" was Pammy Monroe. Pammy was definitely Randy's type; in fact she and Randy had been together for about two years until she left in '83 to take up with some other guy from Bassett. That idiot had managed to get himself sentenced to ten years in prison so now Pammy was back among the Pagans, working her magnificent blue-jean clad rear end hoping someone would notice. Randy noticed. It brought back fond memories and while Randy might have beat the bitch to death when she left, he had different feelings now. Much different. His eyes softened he was smiling showing his clean, gold-capped teeth. He was what passed for charming and it didn't take much to charm Pammy. She made it plain that she wanted Randy. Renee, on the other hand, didn't want anything but relief from the awful pain in her back. She spent her evening eating pain pills, swilling whiskey and sitting morosely in the old Monte Carlo.

By midnight on Saturday, Randy had forgotten all about Renee. He and Pammy made their way into the woods where there was a parked pickup truck. Caught up in the moment, Randy pulled Pammy's blue jeans down to her knees and spun her around to gaze on that large familiar white ass. He bent her over the hood of the truck and began furiously to not just remember old times but to relive them. You might say he relived those old times with true enthusiasm.

In the Monte Carlo, Renee woke up and began looking for Randy. He wasn't that hard to find. Pammy turned out to be a noisy date. Renee saw the goings-on and in a single moment of stunned shock, and, in spite of the agony in her back, she attacked. Randy found himself in a hail storm of blows at the same time Renee went after the compromised Pammy. In a normal situation Pammy could have easily taken Renee but, well, Pammy's jeans were down to her knees and in such a predicament Renee's overwhelming rage was more than the poor Pammy could handle. Pammy fell to the ground so Randy pulled Renee off, carrying her kicking and spitting back to the Monte Carlo. Pammy pulled up her jeans and scurried off into the dark woods laughing and calling back to Renee, "You can have him, dumb bitch!"

Ol' Renee always did have a temper. It was difficult, but Randy managed to force Renee back into the car and drive off toward his farm in Surry County. The farm was on Slate Mountain Road and was in the name of Randy's widowed mother who lived there and looked after the place for him. This was a modern, rambling house attached to a spacious garage and shop where Randy cared for his sizable collection of cars, trucks and motorcycles. It was set on 25 acres far enough back from the public road to avoid the attention of the idle passerby. This is where Randy spent his time and his money. The little house in Martinsville was his residence of record so as not to attract the curiosity of tax agents and law enforcement, but the farm was his home. He had a small cycle repair shop in Martinsville to provide a legitimate occupation and plausible explanation as to where his money came from.

The drive from Hillsville to his own farm that night was miserable. Renee cursed him and beat him with her fists until her back seized up in a colossal spasm of intense agony. Randy had wanted to go back to Martinsville on Sunday, but Renee wasn't up to it; she spent the day in a stupor of pills and alcohol while Randy visited with his mother and tinkered with a motorcycle in his shop.

The following day dawned as a gray foggy Monday morning, Randy and Renee set off before dawn for Martinsville in the big black Monte Carlo. They crossed the Virginia line on 103 and went north into Stuart on Route 8, then East on U.S. Highway 58 where they crashed and smashed at the Spoon Creek Bridge.

I had been a member of JEB Stuart Volunteer Rescue Squad for five years, and on this particular early morning I was asleep when the tones went off: two long notes followed by five short beeps. "Patrick to any available JEB Stuart member. I have a report of a 10-50 (automobile accident) possible PI (personal injury) Highway 58 East at Spoon Creek Bridge. Any available members please respond. Time out 0610."

I really wanted to go back to sleep. Between pulling a calf and arguing with my wife Glenda I had slept three hours that night. Glenda and I had been married sixteen long years. She had been a high school sweetheart and my one and only serious lover. She had stuck with me through college, through veterinary school, and through four years of Army service (much of which was an unaccompanied overseas posting.) Meanwhile, she worked at the jobs a high school graduate could get. She paid the bills while I got an education. The anticipated result would be a "normal" life. I would be a successful veterinarian happy in my work, she would be a happy homemaker. There would be a kid, a house, a car. But when it came to actually living this supposedly "normal" life we realized that through most of our marriage we had been preoccupied with other things: the demands and exhaustion of constant work and study. We had spent little time actually together. We led separate lives while living at the same address. My marriage had become a slow-motion train wreck and having a son didn't help. We both wanted out but neither of us would admit it. Neither of us knew how to fix it nor end it.

In the dark bedroom I pulled on my blue jeans, my western boots, my long drover coat and a broad brim cowboy hat. It was my usual attire; I was mainly a cow doctor in those days, and I owned a small herd of beef cows. After so many years, the clothes felt comfortable and identified me as much as a Pagan's cuts.

"Where are you going? Come back to bed. I'm cold." mumbled Glenda as she struggled to awaken.

"Can't. I got a car wreck at Spoon Creek." I replied, buckling my belt.

"Bullshit. Come back to bed and we'll have sex". That took a long minute of consideration on my part. We may not have been soul mates and we may not have liked each othe,r but she was still a fine looking woman, with, let's say, hidden talents.

"318 to Patrick. 10-76 to the crew hall." It was Anthony Price signing on. The "300" series identified JEB Stuart's Volunteer Rescue Squad and differentiated us from members of other squads in the county. The call numbers 300, 310, 320... signified "units": that is a fully staffed, fully stocked ambulance. The numbers 301 through 309 were reserved for remembering the .45 tucked into his belt. Then, "Goddam! The gun!" Now Randy McAllen was talking out loud. "And the dope!

Dumb bastard, you're sittin' here with a gun and a pocket full of dope waitin' on all the cops in the world to show up." He had forgotten about the baggie of crystal meth still inside the pocket of his cuts; now he forgot, as best he could, about his pain. It didn't matter if he lived or died or how serious his injuries might be; he was a convicted felon and a member of the Pagan's Motorcycle Club. He was in possession of a controlled substance and a gun. If he survived, the state was just going to bury him alive in prison. Forever. His thoughts turned back to the gun. Better to blow his own brains out. Save everybody a lot of trouble. His thoughts were broken by the sound of Renee crying.

Poor Renee Kits had crashed through the windshield hit the upper cement rail of the bridge and bounced back into the road landing beside the right front wheel of the ill-fated Monte Carlo. It should have killed her; but she hit things just right, she had plenty of natural padding, so she was lucky. Unfortunately, while her injuries were not fatal, they were nonetheless serious and painful. Lying on her back on the wet pavement Renee began to cry. At first, she was whimpering, then she began to squall and cry out "I don't wanta die!" and then, "I didn't do it! It wasn't my fault" when, of course she did do it and it certainly was her fault.

Immobilized by his own injuries and pain, Randy didn't want to hear Renee. At all. In fact, it would have suited Randy if she'd been killed outright. Not only did she cause the wreck by deliberately crashing the car into the bridge, but she had seriously injured them both. Because of the bag of meth and the gun, she may even have contributed to sending Randy back to prison for life. Angrily he decided that she had just ruined his whole life. "Shut up, dumb whore!" Randy tried to say but his breathing was so compromised that he spoke only in a halting whisper. Renee couldn't hear him over her own screams, but Randy went on anyway. "I'm gonna tell 'em it's your goddam dope and your goddam gun! How you like that? I'm gonna throw you under the bus! I'm gonna tell 'em you're the biggest drug dealer in Virginia! Yeah, Bitch! I'm gonna tell 'em you sell so much shit they call you 'Miss Wal-Mart'! How you like that?" The little speech had exhausted Ol' Randy which left him so short of breath he actually thought he might die plus Renee's cries were annoying him to death.

He considered shooting her with the pistol through the right car door. "Let me get this gun out and I'll put you out of your misery! I'll shoot your dumb ass!" But Randy had trouble moving his arm and he figured that if he shot at someone he couldn't see, he'd probably miss or just wound her and then she'd really be yelling and screaming and, after all, this wasn't exactly Randy's lucky day. There was one good thing about it, Renee attracted attention to herself. When the gray-uniformed State Trooper showed up, he looked wordlessly at Randy then disappeared to check on screaming Renee. Motionless Randy appeared dead or dying while Renee clearly was not.

The first person to show any interest in Randy was Rusty Wilcox. Rusty was a big, red-haired freckled kid who graduated from Patrick County High with no plans and no prospects. He couldn't afford college and he didn't want to go into the army. He got a job at Dairy Queen and kept living with his parents. I talked him into running with JEB Stuart because we needed all the help we could get, and he seemed smart enough and strong enough to be a real asset to the squad. More importantly, he really cared. He quickly became one of our most active and enthusiastic volunteers. He was taking the EMT class with Carolyn, but he didn't yet have a radio. He had heard the radio traffic on his scanner that misty September morning and had rushed to the scene to see what he could do to help. What he did was to poke his head through Randy's window and, in the words of the EMT course, "reassure the patient." Randy remained motionless, concentrating on each breath. It became increasingly difficult to breathe. "We have an ambulance on the way, Sir. We're going to get you out of here and transport you to the emergency room. Everything's going to be fine. Just relax..." said young Rusty Wilcox earnestly to the seriously injured, tough as nails Pagan whose main concern was the pistol stuck in his britches and a serious amount of crystal meth in his pocket.

Randy squinted and rolled his eyes to fix the kid with his most intimidating stare. Randy was not reassured at all. In fact, he was thinking "Jesus I wish this dumb bastard would go somewhere and fuck himself." Rusty stayed at the window staring at the injured man. He did shut up. Something about the eyes. Those black eyes. The eyes creeped him out, and he thought it better to keep quiet and not piss this victim off.

squad crews watched the chopper disappear off to the south. Within the hour, Mr. Randy McAllen was in surgery and eventually, he would be discharged. He would never be "good as new" but he would be better than he deserved. And alive. The system had worked well for Mr. McAllen

We started walking back to the ER to clean up the mess and recover equipment, I drifted over next to Nedra. She always wore a white nurse's dress with the traditional cap. Rarely did Nedra ever wear scrubs which had become the standard for most nurses, and never ever did she look anyway but beautiful. "Good job." she said, without looking at me while lighting her cigarette.

"What are you doing here this morning, anyway? I thought you were on second forever." I was very fond of this lady and I tried to see her at every opportunity. If they changed her schedule, I might have to modify my habits accordingly.

"Macy Reilly called in sick again and it was my turn to work a double shift. I've been at this place since four o'clock yesterday afternoon. My head is swimming and my eyes are burning and I'm going straight home to bed."

"Can I go too?" I asked grinning.

Nedra stopped walking, turned toward me and blew a long stream of gray cigarette smoke in my face. "No." Then she walked off.

I was thinking now about the plastic bag of powder in my pants and the big gun in my boot; I figured the bag contained some controlled substance and the gun, well the gun was a concealed weapon on hospital property. That's two felony charges. I reckon most people would have handed the gun and the bag over to the trooper. Not me. Except in cases of an obvious threat to someone's safety, I didn't think it was right for the Rescue Squad to conduct warrantless searches for law enforcement. Hell, more than a few of my patients had dope in their possession and almost every adult in Patrick County carried a gun on them. If we started turning our patients in to the law, pretty soon, folks would stop calling for help when they needed it.

I thought about throwing the dope and the gun into a dumpster when I noticed that sitting on the brick wall outside the ER was a solitary grizzled Pagan soaking up the sun like an old bull frog on a rock. I knew something about the Pagans. My band had played at some of their parties. We never played *Free Bird*. After I had noticed the colors on my patient Randy, I knew he was a Pagan.

I sauntered over to the seated Pagan. He was a very large man. He ignored me, staring off into the middle distance. "Excuse me. Did, uh, did you know that guy?" I gestured to the helicopter field. He continued his stony stare, but I thought I detected an almost imperceptible flicker in his eyes. "Anyway, he gave me this," and I stuck my hand in my pants and pulled out the plastic bag. Now the Pagan was trying not to laugh. I took out my pocket knife, opened it and cut a big hole in the bag letting the powder loose to fall on the grass. I'd seen the damage this poison could do to people and I wasn't about to give it back, but I wanted somebody to know I didn't keep it for myself or sell it. "He also gave me this." I reached into my boot and pulled out the .45. Now the old Pagan watched me intently. The weapon was a good condition M-1911 Colt ACP, not the M-1911-A of World War II but an earlier model. I removed the magazine and then the bullets from the magazine and put them in my pocket. I cleared the weapon by pulling back the slide. I let the slide slam back with a loud crash, lowered the hammer and handed the pistol butt first to the Pagan. This Pagan known as "Blade" said nothing, but he did nod his head, slowly and nearly imperceptibly.

I didn't know it at the time, of course, but I'd just saved my own life. Coiled and hidden in Patrick County were rattlesnakes. Deadly poisonous things, evil things born of greed and ready to strike.

CHAPTER TWO

The Volunteers

"Where's the horse?" I asked as I jumped out of my jeep. I was late getting to the Surry County farm of my fiend Duke Satterfield.

"In his stall. Back there in that little barn." said Duke, a retired firefighter and Paramedic from Forsyth County. As a young man he had spent some time playing professional baseball in the Carolina League. He never hit the "majors," but the big man still looked and moved like the ball player he was.

As I got to the stall, I noticed the stall door was open and lying in the doorway was the head of an obviously dead horse. "He's dead." I blurted.

"Damn right he's dead!" roared my client. "Dead, dead, dead! He's graveyard dead! Dead as a doornail dead! Dead as four o'clock dead! Been dead so long, he's practically road- kill! Oh, but I called the famous veterinarian. Hours ago! My old horse was at death's door and the veterinarian pulled him through…the door that is!"

I was a little nervous. In those days, if your clients thought you screwed-up they wouldn't sue you. They might beat the hell out of you. But instead of hitting me he started laughing. He slapped me on the shoulder and said "You ought to see the look on your face, Doc. Don't worry. I ain't mad. Hell, he was forty-two years old and he was way past saving. If he had been alive when you got here, I was going to have you shoot him anyway. I've had my fun for today. Come on to the house and we'll have a drink. My Uncle Bascombe give me four quarts of corn liquor yesterday and I ain't tasted any of it yet. Ol' Bascombe knows how to make that stuff. It burns going down and then it tastes sweet." I found myself surrounded by a huge arm.

"I don't know if I can. It's been a long day and I need to get…"

"Now you're making me mad. You ain't gonna drink with me after lettin' my old horse die without benefit of a bullet?" The big man stepped back from me and expressed mock offense.

"Well, if you're going to be that way about it, I don't see how I can really refuse."

Community, a sense of responsibility that will compel the volunteers, to do what they have to do. It's like that now. When there is a bad wreck or a big house fire, the funeral home doesn't take care of it. We do. All of us. We pitch in and do what we can, but the difference is that we are doing it without the training and equipment.

"Thank you, gentlemen for your time." Bertha knew she hadn't said enough to defeat the Russell's but she didn't know what more she could say.

"And we thank you." said the Honorable Chairman of the Board. "Is there anyone else who would like to be heard on this matter before we vote?"

"Yes, your Honor." said a strange, small older man from the back of the room. "At the pleasure of the Board, I think I have something to offer to the discussion." Eyes turned to the stranger. He was thin to the point of frailty with a drawn wrinkled face. He had deep-set blue eyes and a shock of glowing white hair. Hair that would have been visible in the dark.

"Who are you, sir? State your name and residence, please." replied the Honorable Chairman.

"I am Dr. Edward Kallam from Richmond. I am the newly appointed Director of Emergency Services for the Commonwealth of Virginia. I was asked by Bertha Jones to come down here and assist in developing a volunteer rescue squad. I think it is important for the Board to know that your vote on this question is irrelevant. There is new legislation requiring that all localities provide emergency services for their citizens and there are regulations governing the equipment and procedures used. This legislation makes the Funeral home hearse as an ambulance a thing of the past. Like it or not, you are obligated to set up some sort of proper ambulance service."

"Thank you for your opinion Dr....uhm... well... uh...Doctor. (The Chairman couldn't remember the doctor's name.) The Board will consider it." Then all five members of the esteemed Board looked to the end of the bench where the County Administrator sat. The administrator closed his eyes and pursed his lips. Then he slowly shook his head. The fix was in. The signal given. It would be a unanimous "no" vote on volunteer rescue squads. The Russell family would again get what they wanted state law notwithstanding.

At that moment Mr. B. C. Weathers had a heart attack. The big man stood up suddenly, puffing like a freight train, gasping for every bit of air.

He instantly became drenched in sweat. Between gasps he panted "God Almighty!... I can't breathe!...Help me somebody!...I can't breathe!" The cocker spaniel eyes, usually drooped and sleepy were now wild; nearly popping out of their sockets and roving around the room searching for help. With a heavy thud, he collapsed back into his seat. The only sound in the room was his rasping, loud efforts to move air.

Dr. Kallam went instantly to the side of the afflicted Mr. Weathers but with no tools there was little he could do. He loosened the tie and ripped open the shirt exposing the hairy heaving chest, wet with sweat.

Dr. Kallam completed a cursory examination and then made the classic announcement: "We've got to get this man to a hospital!" The assembled crowd, which had been up to that time frozen in a collective open-mouthed stupor, suddenly sprang into action. There was no ambulance and no hearse. Two men grabbed each large leg, one man was under each shoulder and a seventh man cradled the sweat-soaked head. With much straining, grunting and muttering, they carried Mr. Weathers down the old courthouse steps and placed him in the back seat of a Cadillac belonging to one of the board members.

Mr. B. C. Weathers would survive and live another two years, suffering at least three additional cardiac events.

The next evening, the Board of Supervisors met to take care of their unfinished business. They were expected to vote against any funding or support of a volunteer rescue squad, but an odd thing happened. The Rescue Squad and Bertha Jones won the vote by a 3 to 2. As powerful and feared as the Russell Family was, there was a higher power. In the eyes of the three board members, God himself had stricken Mr. B. C. Weathers to send a sign to the Board.

Signs from God Almighty are carefully observed here; not to be ignored. JEB Stuart Volunteer Rescue Squad became a reality in Patrick County by dent of a serendipitous heart attack.

Later the three board members who voted against the Russell family failed to win re-election to the Board of Supervisors.

I volunteered not just to run calls as an EMT but also, it turned out, to be Captain of the squad. In those days, you volunteered to be Captain by not showing up for the meeting during which officers were elected and you and tracked down Ralphie's nose. Slowly Ralphie turned and began to stagger about the saw- mill, leaning over one piece of equipment after another banging them with both hands. He began a strange, high pitched wail. It was not a typical human sound. It was chilling and unnerving. The cry of death. It was more than Carl could stand. Still holding the pistol in his now limp hand, Carl walked away. He walked across his farm to the old house that had belonged to his grandparents. The house was abandoned, and was in the process of crumbling, but there was enough of it left that Carl could sit on the front porch. Deep into memories of a childhood with Ralphie; memories now forever tainted with sorrow and regret due to a quick thoughtless act with a small pistol. There were no more wails from the sawmill site.

It was a quiet, fresh spring morning. An anonymous woman heard the gun shot then called the Patrick County Sheriff's office and requested an ambulance. "Something bad has happened down at the saw- mill."

Jarrell Price, Larry Cane and Rusty Wilcox answered the call. Jarrell and Larry had been EMT's for less than a year. Rusty had only a CPR card even though he was enrolled in EMT class. On the way to the scene the three usually exuberant young men were quietly subdued. With no more to go on than an address, they had no idea what to expect. Sawmill injuries can be some of the most gory and difficult cases to handle and frequently involve amputations. They found the saw- mill deserted and literally as silent as a grave.

"Maybe somebody called this in just to screw with us." remarked Rusty.

"And maybe they didn't." answered Jarrell. "Y'all be really careful and keep your eyes open. We don't know what we got here. Could be a violent scene with a perpetrator still here. He might decide to do us too." Jarrell was practically whispering.

The three fanned out, searching for their patient. There was no talking as they crept about among the stacks of boards and the machinery, including two large skidders. They were constantly moving their eyes over the scene. All three felt the tingling of fear mixed with excitement that all EMS providers become familiar with. They each knew that this could go very wrong very fast.

"Blood!" called Larry. He had found a small amount of fresh blood on some of the stacked lumber.

"Feet!" called Rusty. There were a pair of boots sticking out from under one of the huge saws. The crew assembled next to the saw, looking down at the motionless Wolverine boots attached to blue jean-clad legs. "Y'all reckon he's alive?"

"I don't know, but we've got to find out." Jarrell grabbed one of the exposed boots and shook it robustly "Are you OK? Are you OK?" Jarrell called out the usual greeting that ambulance personnel use when first meeting the victim, especially an unresponsive victim. There was no answer because Ralphie wasn't OK at all. He was dead. "One of us has to crawl under there and check him out."

"Not me" said Larry. "Suppose the Dude ain't dead. Suppose he's got a gun and he's just waitin' to…"

"Me neither" interrupted Rusty. "I'm OK with dead guys but it's a little creepy to be in tight places with 'em."

Jarrell already had the flashlight and stethoscope out of his junk bag and was squirming under the heavy steel frame of the saw. Jarrell was a thin man, yet he scraped his back as he writhed into the narrow space. Ralphie was lying on his front with his head turned to the left, facing Jarrell. It was instantly apparent to the young EMT that Ralphie was dead. His skin was tan-gray and cold, he wasn't breathing, his eyes were open pupils dilated and unresponsive to light. There was a bullet hole between his eyes.

Rescue Squad personnel may not "pronounce" a patient dead. If they are certain about it, they may "announce" that the person is deceased. After checking carefully for a carotid pulse and using his stethoscope to check for a heartbeat that wasn't there, Jarrell backed out of the crawl space. "You guys see a gun?" Jarrell asked rhetorically. "Me neither. It's probably a homicide. People rarely shoot themselves between the eyes when there's no gun. Let's follow our own tracks back to the unit. Don't touch anything and keep your eyes open. The shooter may still be here, and he may still be pissed off." They were jogging back to the ambulance. "Larry. Get on the radio and tell dispatch what we got. Randy. You come with me and help me put up the tape." In those days, if an ambulance crew came upon a possibly violent or suspicious death, the procedure was to first determine that the victim was in fact dead. Then they were charged with "securing the scene."

We carried several rolls of bright yellow crime scene tape marked in big black letters **POLICE LINE DO NOT CROSS.**

A small amount of the EMT course addressed the proper actions to take at homicide scenes. Tape off the perimeter. Don't touch anything. Never pick up any weapons at the scene unless they pose an immediate threat to safety. Don't talk to bystanders and if you have any thought that the murderer may still be on the scene; leave. In those days, once law enforcement arrived, we had to stay with the deceased body until it was released by the investigators at which time, we were to carefully transport the body to the funeral home of the family's choice and await the medical examiner. In Virginia, all violent or suspicious deaths require a complete autopsy by a licensed medical examiner. Sometimes, by the time the State Police van drove down from Salem and completed their work, we had spent the night at the scene. Ralphie's body was released at around 6:00 p.m. The three "kids" were greatly relieved.

Carl left his seat on the porch and drove to the Sheriff's office where he surrendered still holding the small cheap pistol in his right hand. The devil's right hand. Carl plead guilty and was sentenced to ten years in prison. The Commonwealth could not begin to punish him as much as he punished himself for his "act of Caine" that earliest of biblical murders also involving two brothers.

There were four women in the squad.

Maggie Engel was quiet, dignified and patrician, which well she should have been since her husband was the president of the local bank. Maggie was from Huntersville, North Carolina. A small town, north of Charlotte and had studied pre-law at Duke University. She met and fell in love with Harry Engel, an economics major from Stuart. As she would say to her friends, they got married and moved to "Where's That?" Virginia to raise a son and a daughter. Once the children left the nest, Maggie became bored and tried first helping out at the church, then the school, then finally, the rescue squad. The rescue squad must have cured her boredom. She eventually ran calls for twenty years. Maggie Engel always had her hair combed neatly back in a bun and she was never seen without makeup. Not a lot of makeup, but just enough. She was thin and at first glance, gave the false impression of fragility, but as is common in certain Southern women, she was not so much fragile crystal as tempered steel.

Her thin face was dominated by a large beak-like nose. Her mouth was thin lipped and delicate. Her eyes were a piercing hazel and quite capable of casting a withering stare when needed. Overall, she looked like what she was: an attractive, well-bred, well-educated, high-class lady. I often wondered what would have happened if she had finished Duke and gone to law school. I decided she may well have wound up as a judge, similar to Justice Susie Sharpe in North Carolina, to whom she bore more than a passing resemblance.

Carolyn Miller on the other hand was a loud, laughing, good-time girl who became the center of attention (particularly male attention) at any party or bar. Her hair always needed a good brushing and her general appearance was disheveled. Carolyn and Maggie hated each other. Nobody seemed to know exactly what started the feud. Some say Carolyn got too friendly with Maggie's husband at a party one night. Basically, it was a case of two strong personalities sharing the same space. They were like two old cats sitting at opposite ends of a sofa growling at each other, waiting for the opportunity to attack and vanquish the hated rival. It became a problem because if one signed on to run a call, the other would stay home, even if it delayed the response time and jeopardized the call itself.

So, I took them to lunch. When they saw each other, the lunch nearly didn't happen!

Maggie arrived first and the two of us were looking at the menu and making small talk. I didn't tell either of them that the other had been invited. I figured neither of them would have showed up.

"What's *she* doing here?" called out Carolyn loudly as soon as she entered the restaurant.

"Eating lunch, I hope." replied Maggie quietly without turning her head but her face was flushed.

"I'm surprised you'd want to be seen with a low life like me."

"Good point. I may just go." and Maggie began collecting her things to leave.

"No, no, no. Please. Don't leave. Carolyn, come and join us. Ladies, please for a short time let's put it all away. Please." I was begging and pleading but I also knew I was in real trouble and if things didn't improve, they both might quit the squad.

and he hated me. When he wasn't calling me the "dog medic" he called me "that fag" which I gathered was a term he used for anyone who didn't agree with his stupid ideas. He criticized the Rescue Squad and everything else in the County. If we had just asked old Walter, everything would have worked perfectly. Yeah, but just try asking him what to do *before* the fact! Walter the genius would become Walter the deaf-mute. He was the king of twenty-twenty hindsight. I shouldn't have felt like I did. It was wrong. Walter was a willing volunteer and a great driver and one more hand on the stretcher. He was less damaging because nobody really paid much attention to anything he said, but I couldn't help myself. If he had quit the squad, I'd have been awful slow to talk him into reconsidering. Of course, that blowhard would be the last guy to ever quit the squad. I kept my opinions to myself and secretly hoped he'd move to Myrtle Beach and sunbathe himself to death.

There were twelve of us who ran the calls in 1989. Two black guys, six white guys, four women, rich and not so rich, educated formally and educated practically, young, old and in between. Looking at it, my crew was a cross section of the county population in general, but for all our differences we came together to run the calls and serve our community. We were the drivers, the EMT's and the attendants who first cared for the sick and wounded in Patrick County 24 hours a day, seven days a week. There were all kinds of situations in all kinds of weather. In those days, not one of us received a dime. We were unpaid volunteers. Nobody was in it for the money. We were here because we were decent people doing a decent thing, and to this day, I have the highest regard for every one of them, even, grudgingly, old Walter Mayhew.

Now, while the volunteers weren't paid, everything else had to be. An ambulance cost approximately $65,000.00 in those days. Then there were maintenance expenses, fuel, insurance, supplies and rent (yes, we paid rent on the shack). It came to about $25,000.00 in expenses each year, which doesn't seem like a lot of overhead for any business unless you consider that there was no income. In 1989 all services provided to the public by the rescue squad were free. To get money, we depended on private donations, state and local government grants, loans, and fundraisers. It was a constant scramble to stay ahead of insolvency. Bertha Jones served as our Treasurer. At some point during every meeting, all eyes would turn to poor Bertha for the Treasurer's report; and every month poor Bertha would shuffle her stack of papers, take in a deep breath, blow it out slowly with puffed cheeks and regard the documents before her with the same mixture of sadness and disgust that one might reserve for looking at a run-over dead dog. There would be a moment of reverent silence, she would look up, adjust her glasses and with a severe frown announce to the membership, "Well, we're broke." This monthly ritual never varied. Fortunately, people in Patrick County are used to being broke and are practiced at scrambling after dollars.

In most Rescue Squads and Fire Departments, fund raising falls to the Auxiliary which is typically made up of the spouses. Among our little group of twelve, only four of us were married. Anthony Price's wife was busy enough with children and grandchildren, Carolyn Miller's husband was disabled and was too busy watching TV and swilling beer, a bank president is unlikely to organize a bake sale, and my wife, Glenda wished the rescue squad would go broke so I would be at home more often. The burden of fund-raising fell on we hapless volunteers, which meant not only did we spend time running calls, but also begging for money. Carolyn Miller with her enthusiasm, became our fund-raising leader.

Sometimes we did, actually beg. Some of us would go to the clubs; Rotary, Ruritans, Lions, etc. and talk about what the squad did and how badly we needed help. Typically, these service organizations were quite generous. Many citizens thought the ambulances belonged to the County and were staffed by paid County employees. The squads were private non-profit corporations governed by strict tax laws and subject to close public scrutiny. Essentially, the squads belonged to the community. The Board of Trustees and the Line Officers managed them as a public trust. Once people understood this setup, most were more than willing to help. There was a tremendous public relations benefit by having we volunteers give dinner presentations.

One night, Anthony Price and Walter Mayhew spoke to the Stuart Rotary Club. Anthony gave the standard appeal for help. Then the president of the Club asked Walter if he wanted to say a few words. Anthony was shocked when Walter leapt to the lectern. He thought Walter had come along for the free meal and drinks.

to protect their eyes and SCBA (self-contained breathing apparatuses) to protect them from the deadly poisonous gases present in smoke. They also have hoses to beat down flames and cool things off. I knew it was stupid not to wait and let the firemen go after Larry and Mathew but well...hell...

I leapt up the few steps to the front door and plunged through the open door into that thick deadly smoke. I couldn't see and I couldn't breathe. What a stupid situation I had placed myself in and the increasing smoke meant the whole damn thing could break into flames at any second; but no sooner did I enter the trailer than something hit me and knocked me out into the freezing night and down the steps. It was Larry carrying four-year old Mathew.

The fire truck was now on scene and swarming firemen were connecting hoses and heading toward the trailer when the whole thing exploded in a bright orange fire ball. As I said, like a match head. I felt the heat on my back as I pushed Larry into the yard and away from the fire. Ed was already dragging Janice and the other children away. Everything stopped as soon as Janice saw little Mathew in Larry's arms. Janice Johnston engulfed the four year- old with her large arms, crying and praising the Almighty. I don't think I ever saw anyone so happy or cry so much.

"He was right inside the door. Right there in the hallway holding his teddy bear. I couldn't believe it!" said Larry Cane with a broad grin on his face.

"It doesn't matter! You were lucky but that was a stupid goddam thing for you to do! We could all be dead right now!" I was yelling at him and waving my arms around.

"Yeah, I know." laughed Larry Cane. Rusty Wilcox was now patting his buddy on the back and they were both laughing, laughing in relief and laughing at me.

"Don't you ever do anything that stupid again! You hear me?" I knew I was wasting my breath. Ed stood behind me looking down and shaking his head as if to wonder what we could possibly do with a crew such as this.

Now both Larry and Rusty stopped laughing and pulled themselves to attention. They looked serious and saluted me. It didn't last long before they were both again doubled over in laughter.

"Ah forget it. You'd do the same thing again and so would I."

From his laughter I heard Larry say, "Damn straight we would, Doc."

Once his mother was through smothering him with love, we checked out little Mathew, put him on high flow oxygen and hauled the entire family to the hospital. The Red Cross would meet us there. With some help from generous citizens, the family bought a new home and moved in by July.

I'm not sure how well the system worked in this case, but I certainly nodded to the Almighty. Several times.

The family returned to Stuart. There were fewer loose women, less alcohol and not so many gambling opportunities. Getting him out of Danville helped but the playboy father still pursued his vices in Patrick County. The boy grew up as a lonely only child. Surrounded by servants in a huge house in the middle of town with any amenity or toy his doting mother could find to bestow on him.

When of age, he was dutifully enrolled in the Stuart Elementary school. For the first time he was no longer sheltered, for the first time the boy was exposed to other children. As we know, children can be cruel. A chant commonly heard on the playground when the boy was outside with his class was:

Peg, Peg he's got no foot
Ain't got nothin' but a
Peg of wood!

As bad as his handicap was, in a group that valued physical good looks and athletic ability, the boy had neither. He was tall and awkward. His face was thin with a very large nose that gave him a bird-like appearance and not just any bird but that of a great blue heron. The large black eyes were set close to the beak and bored-in on people as a heron might look at a fish. His hesitant movements and long thin hands, legs and arms further contributed to the resemblance. As painful as the nick name "Peg" was, he soon picked up another: "Stork." On top of his body was a mass of unruly black hair. Then there was a problem with his nose: it didn't work well. As large as it was, his nose was constantly stopped up which made him breathe through his mouth and talk with an unpleasant nasal tone. His teeth were large and for all the advantages of his home, dental care was not included. The boy's teeth were dirty.

Public school could be expected to be a miserable experience for such a child and miserable he was. He spent most of his time hiding in out of the way corners crying and hating. Hating all those cruel children who called him "Peg" or "Stork" and soon hating all children, all people. He wanted to hurt them all. Make them feel the misery he lived with. He wanted them to suffer as he had. Then came the first of two early lessons in his life. Yes, he was ugly, tall and ungainly all inherited from his great grandfather, the Colonel. From his paternal grandmother (a particularly homely, aloof and cold woman) he inherited brains. Fabulous brains. He had a photographic memory and a rare ability to quickly grasp difficult concepts. He found that knowing the right answers won him respect, if not from the school yard bullies, then at least from the teachers. It was also better to hide in corners with a book than to just hide and cry. He would lose himself in books. His mother, barely literate herself, delighted in buying him anything he wanted. Desperate to please her only child, once she found that he became excited by a new book, she purchased him a library full of them. The first big lesson was that with brains, he could build a protective wall of books around himself. Education and knowledge, a shield, protecting him from the cruel children who valued looks and athletic ability while calling him "Peg" and "Stork."

His mother didn't understand her strange son. He was unlike anyone she had ever known. Servants looked after his basic needs, but for the most part, the boy preferred to be alone and untouched. Mother was quite young and very beautiful, but she found herself by the accident of pregnancy in a family of unattractive, cold wealthy people, not at all like her own large, loving, close but poor background. She was used to mothers hugging their children and children who sought out such attention. Father passed through the home sometimes, but he was mostly absent gambling, drinking and womanizing. The wife and son were to him as the expensive furniture in his sitting room. When away he scarcely thought about them. When he was at home, he might use them. The furniture didn't interfere with his pursuits and neither did his wife and son.

For his fifth grade the boy was sent away to boarding school in Maryland. He certainly didn't mind. No one taunted him or made fun of him there. These students were from wealthy families and had heard that this tall ungainly one-footed child might be the wealthiest of them all. Here was the second major lesson: money brings respect and power like nothing else can. If education would be a shield from the world then money would be a sword to carve out his desires from a hostile world. Academic honors and awards came easily to him and he developed a self-confidence he had never enjoyed before. He still hated his fellow pupils. He might have been awkward, and ugly, and handicapped but he was smarter than they were, he was richer than they were, and that realization gave him

him and turned on his red flashing lights. Ernie pulled onto the shoulder and flung himself to the ground screaming and crying, "Y'all got me! You got me goddam it! Oh, Sweet Jesus…just take me on to jail!" After finding the whiskey in the truck, the astonished officer did just that. The officer had stopped Ernie because he noticed the rear license plate was missing. That was all. The trooper had no intention of searching the truck.

Sheriff Drew Watson dutifully locked up his incredibly stupid cousin in the Patrick County Jail. Drew thanked the State Policeman for his help in cleaning up Patrick County. Later Drew went to see the Judge. The Judge observed that it was hard to guess what that stupid bastard Ernie might say. It would be better for everybody if he just killed himself. That night, in the Patrick County Jail Ernie Tutterow supposedly did just that. The Sheriff investigated the coroner signed the paper. Another tragic suicide.

By 1970, the illegal whiskey business wasn't as profitable anyway. Most of the customers were black residents within the inner cities who didn't pay much and had little appreciation for a quality product. If you were looking for a cheap drunk; white lightning wasn't that cheap. Sugar prices had increased, and the stores were full of cheap wines and beer. There were government taxed brands of whiskey that sold for less than illegal bootleg. Yes, illegal alcohol had been good to Patrick County and especially good to Butch Russell, Drew Watson and the Judge. But times were changing.

A new illegal product was on the horizon, a product with the promise of much greater profits: marijuana. Starting in the mid-sixties there developed an exploding demand for this weed in institutions of higher education and urban centers. Despite its rural location, Patrick County is within an hour's drive of six colleges, universities and their surrounding urban centers. While there has always been some home-grown (popularly referred to as "skunk weed") this weed was looked down upon and considered to be less potent and less sophisticated. Among the affluent, there was an acquired taste for this product from such countries as Columbia, Panama, and Mexico. The problem was getting it from there to here. After all, marijuana possession is illegal under state and federal law. Illegal but profitable; and where there is enough profit, certain people will become very clever at breaking the law. The Judge was certainly in that group.

Patrick County offered numerous secluded cow pastures for airstrips with the added advantage of thoroughly corrupt local law enforcement. Landing little airplanes in Winston-Salem or Greensboro might attract attention, but in Patrick County, you could do it with impunity. So, the little airplanes began to fly regularly into Patrick, landing on improvised airfields belonging to Butch Russell or Drew Watson. The bales of Columbian Green and Panama Red marijuana were put into dump trucks, covered with wood mulch and hauled south to wholesale distribution sites. The small aircraft would circle the landing fields in the dead of night. The waiting dump trucks would turn on the head lights to assist the landing. The pilots were all extremely competent, well-paid and daring. The airplane would be on the ground for a few minutes while the cargo was transferred to the trucks and then off the little plane went, disappearing into the covering blackness of the night. The dump trucks disappeared as well, heading toward a landscaping service in North Carolina that served as a wholesale distribution center for decorative trees, flowers and now marijuana! The product would be re-packaged and distributed. But not as wood mulch.

As if the thriving business of smuggling marijuana wasn't enough, another lucrative opportunity presented itself. A small duffle bag filled with Central American powdered cocaine could easily be carried along in the same little airplane. The value of that bag of was more than the marijuana and more than the airplane that carried it. As major crime goes, the scheme was relatively risk free for the "Stuart Boys" as the Judge, Butch Russell and Drew Watson came to be known. The only partner they had was a British national who lived in the Caribbean and lined up Central American suppliers, airplanes and pilots. For his trouble, he took enough money from the top of the cash payments for the "product" to buy his own island. The dump truck workers were hired by intermediaries and had no idea who they worked for. Huge amounts of cash came back via couriers to be hauled back in the little planes after the Stuart Boys removed their sizable cut. The Judge and his associates kept their hands clean. They never touched the "product" and the money came to them by, let's say, secure hidden transactions. It seemed like a safe way to make a lot of illegal money.

County?? A series of events could have been set in motion and could have ended with all three disgraced, impoverished and imprisoned. Most people would have accepted their good fortune graciously and reckoned that enough is enough, but then, there is never enough.

When the door of drug smuggling closes as too risky another door may open that leads not to dealing in illegal commodities like untaxed whiskey and drugs, but rather into illegal money. The Judge and Butch Russell's daddy had been the two original organizers of the Patrick County Hospital. Over the years, Butch and the Judge had acquired the shares from their partners. By 1979 they completely owned the non-profit hospital. There was a hospital Board of Trustees to satisfy IRS requirements, but the Judge made sure that there were no troublemakers on the Board, just solid citizens. Dumb but solid. Butch was the Board Chairman. Now while the Judge and Butch controlled the hospital from behind the scenes and while Butch and the Judge received a profit from their non-profit hospital, they hid their ownership and very few in the county knew who exactly owned the hospital. The commonly accepted fiction was that the community or the Patrick County government owned the hospital or that the hospital somehow owned itself. The Judge knew full well who owned the hospital and the Judge knew an opportunity when he saw one.

On October 15, 1970, the United States Congress passed, and President Richard Nixon signed the Organized Crime Control Act of 1970 including the Racketeer Influenced and Corrupt Organizations Act known as RICO. They said it was not directed against criminal organizations led by those whose names ended in vowels. But of course, it was. A wide-ranging bill, RICO gave law enforcement new powerful tools to investigate and charge those involved in large-scale organized crime.

One result of the law was that banks (anxious not to be included as part of a criminal enterprise) became fastidious about reporting cash transactions over $10,000.00 to the IRS. This had the effect of rendering criminally derived large cash assets nearly worthless. You wouldn't put it in the bank. If one had a box filled with millions of dollars in cash derived from some illegal activity; it might be better than nothing, but it would be far from usable money. A person couldn't buy a great car with it, you couldn't buy a house with it, or a Lear Jet, or a business without the IRS demanding to know a legitimate source of the funds. So, a whole new criminal industry was created: money laundering; a method of converting large amounts of ill-gotten cash into legally usable money. The going rate for this service was about 33% profit off the top. It hadn't been a big deal to the Stuart Boys because they owned the bank. They were still small time compared to other criminals.

Crime, efficiently conducted, can generate huge amounts of cash. Prostitution, gambling, drug-dealing and extortion were all examples of crime in the northeast corridor of the United States; and there were no more efficient crime conductors than the infamous Gambino Family.

Their huge cash profits were transported to Caribbean nations and legally deposited into bogus accounts a process known as "placement". Sometimes the cash was transported in cash-filled airplanes, and sometimes by human mules. Next, the money, no longer in cash, was traded in phony stock sales between phony and sometimes not phony companies; a process known as "layering". This made the money very hard to trace. Finally, the money would be transferred back to the States by another "phony" stock sale or other contrived business transaction, eventually coming back as "clean" money to the original criminal owner, a process known as "integration". Presto! The dirty cash was now nice, clean money ready to spend.

The Judge noticed that the money laundering schemes using private businesses such as brokerage firms, diamond dealers and pizza parlors had to pay private business taxes. Taxes represented a not inconsiderable line item of overhead. Certain transactions conducted by non-profits are tax exempt.

So, the Judge made some calls and soon found himself meeting in a lawyer's office high in the Chrysler building in New York City with four well-dressed "gentlemen" who didn't hand out business cards. The discussion was indirect and imprecise. A recording would not have detected anything illegal. The well-dressed gentlemen informed the Judge that a Hospital Administrator would be provided, and that the job of this administrator would be to "facilitate the arrangements." The Judge, in turn, was required to protect this administrator from any annoyance. Near the end of the meeting one of the well-dressed "gentlemen" gazed impassively at the tall Judge from the South and said, "We do trust your assurances that you have complete control and that at no time will there be any…let's say, unwelcome interference." The Judge knew a threat when he heard it. Wolves now confronted the heron, and for a fleeting moment, it occurred to the Judge that he might be in over his head. It chilled him. But his doubts were overcome by the promise of truly immense profits.

While there was some risk to the arrangement; done correctly using a non-profit entity (such as a small hospital) to avoid paying taxes one could become rich. Very rich. By 1989, Butch Russell and the Judge were each worth over $5 million dollars in net assets. But then, there is never enough.

It was a beautiful spring morning, a bluebird morning some people would say. The call came in that an ambulance was needed to carry an elderly man from the county-line area to the hospital. I knew that because it was mid-morning on a weekday, we would have trouble finding a crew, so I signed on. It was a long time before Anthony Price signed on to drive. Well, that was one to drive and one to watch the old guy in the back. Better than nothing so I went to the crew hall. Anthony already had the ambulance fired up and the red lights flashing. I was surprised when Lucinda Gray suddenly drove up in her car and (typical for her) jumped into the back of the ambulance without saying a word.

"How you today, Morticia?" asked Anthony using the nickname the squad used for this strange pale-skinned waif. She didn't answer. She sat on a jump seat with her knees and elbows drawn close into her body. She pulled a paperback book out of her large bag and began to read, intensely fidgeting as she read. She didn't say a word nor make eye-contact, her body language sent a strong signal: leave me alone and don't bother me. Anthony looked at me, winked and smiled. I smiled back and shook my head slowly. Rescue squad volunteers can include rather eccentric individuals, but Lucinda was truly one of a kind. She continually surprised me with her intelligence, her dedication and her kindness. There was a lot going on beneath her off-putting façade.

Anthony asked if we were ready and without waiting for an answer put the unit in motion. I picked up the radio microphone, "300 to Patrick. 10-76 to the scene."

"10-4, 300. Time out 11:14." Not bad, twelve minutes response time, from the first alert to putting the unit in motion. Not bad for mid-morning on a Wednesday, and we had a complete crew as well. Not bad at all.

It was a twenty-minute ride to the address in northeastern Patrick County. We rode with the flashing red lights, but we didn't use the siren. Traffic was light and every time we used the siren some irate citizen (even in our sparsely populated rural county) would complain that we woke them up, we woke up their child, made their dog bark or frightened their chickens and cows. Besides, no one had said that this was a ripping emergency and Anthony drove the whole way traveling at the legal speed limit.

I envisioned that our patient would be some poor old bed ridden fellow, nearing the end of a long life, the caretakers having called us to take him out of his home for the last time on a one-way trip to the nursing home or the cemetery. Such calls were depressing but on the other hand part of the natural progression of life. All of our lives are lived in stages and in every life, there has to be a final stage. I suppose that those who delay the "final stage" for a complete span of years should count themselves lucky.

The address on County-Line Road was a neat little white house on a well-tended lawn surrounded by well-tended cow pastures surrounded by well-tended fences enclosing sleek Black Angus cows. Anthony pulled the ambulance into the gravel driveway and I called in our arrival to Patrick County dispatch. I grabbed the clipboard and started toward the house.

As I walked across the lawn, I passed a pleasant looking older man in clean bib overalls a clean white shirt and a black unbuttoned sweater. His hands were in his pockets. I didn't recognize the gray-haired man and I assumed he was a neighbor, a friend or a relative. He wasn't. He was the patient.

"How's it going?" I asked as I walked by. His response was to point a .38 snub-nosed Smith and Wesson pistol right between my eyes. I froze. I was at point blank range. If he fired the gun I would die. It was as simple as that. I was close enough to see the bullets in the chambers of the revolver. The gun was loaded all right. People who are trained in such things usually keep their index finger off the trigger and out of the trigger guard until the last instant before shooting. It's a safety measure. This guy's finger was through the trigger guard and wrapped around the trigger. Safety was obviously not a major consideration.

"Uh…not so good I guess." I said as I smiled and tried to look as non-threatening as I could. I would have preferred to grab the pistol away from

It suited me to turn Mr. Leaf over to the deputies. I wasn't very happy with him and maybe a day or two in jail would help his attitude. It had been an unusual call and I was ready to go back to work. Lucinda rode back to the station without saying a word and without reading her book. She looked very sad.

Later we heard that Mr. Leaf had grabbed for a deputy's gun and was killed. At least, that was the story. The Judge bought the farm from Mr. Leaf's widow selling it to a developer of retirement homes for a huge profit.

It was over a month before Lucinda Gray ran another rescue squad call.

The Judge

Great
Blue
Heron

M. Engel 2015

M. Engel 2015

was no hope of resuscitation. The funeral was held Thursday afternoon. Frank Watson became acting Sheriff upon his father's death.

Funerals, especially those of prominent citizens (such as a long-serving sheriff) are important events in Patrick County. If you are an aspiring business leader, a politician or a local government employee, attendance at such an event is almost mandatory. The idea is to see and to be seen. The Judge, however, didn't have to be anywhere he didn't want to be even at the funeral of his old partner in crime but there he was, a tall gaunt figure in a black suit, a heavy black overcoat, bare-headed and apparently unfazed by the cold temperature with the misty February rain.

At the grave side as the huge coffin of the dead Sheriff Watson was lowered into the eternal pit, on one side of the Judge stood Butch Russell and on the other side was a new face in the county: Mr. Alfonse Giordani Fusco the newly arrived administrator of our local R.J. Reynolds hospital. The three stood in somber reverence. The Judge by his presence standing with the two men on either side of him sent a strong message to the community: these men are with the Judge and anyone who opposes them may do so at their own peril. If you messed with this exotic-looking hospital administrator, you may as well mess with the Judge himself.

Mr. Fusco was different from everyone else at the funeral and would have attracted a lot of attention even without his proximity to the Judge. His olive complexion gave him the patina of a constant tan. His hair was jet black, in small curls and shiny. The eyes were black and piercing, the nose straight and fine and the thin lips were as perfect as the large white teeth they covered. He was a "Greek god," an "Adonis." Both expressions had been used to describe the man. Mr. Fusco shook hands with most of the important mourners and engaged them with his intense eyes. He charmed them with his ready white smile radiating sincerity and likeability.

There were several things, however, that Al and the Judge were hiding from the rest of Patrick County. He didn't grow up in Charlotte, N.C. as he claimed but rather New York and Boston. His birth certificate showed a birthplace; New York. He was actually born in Palermo, Sicily. He had, in fact, graduated from Cornell and later from Harvard with an MBA. That was true and was widely reported in the local press. But one major secret Big Al and the Judge kept from the public was that he was a blood member of the Patriarca crime family.

Based in Boston, this was the smallest of the five major families of organized crime. The family was plagued by informants and heavily infiltrated by FBI undercover agents. It wasn't long before the typical criminal pursuits became too risky. In response to this situation, the more realistic and adaptable of the Patriarcas became "bankers to the mob." They handled the money. During the 1980's and '90's that meant money-laundering.

The cash came from criminal activities of the Gambino Family and was taken to Bermuda, the Bahamas and the Cayman Islands. The cash bought shares in bogus companies, which then bought shares in other companies which bought shares in still other companies and so forth. The trail of wealth was difficult if not impossible to follow. Finally, the RJR Patrick County Memorial Hospital wound up owning shares in companies that paid generous dividends: millions of dollars each month. Over a 100% return on the investment each year. What a deal! The hospital then paid the money, all clean and laundered, into Gambino-controlled accounts to pay for non-existent medical services, supplies, equipment, or insurance premiums. In most of these transactions, no tax was owed nor paid.

The checks were all made out to the hospital, arriving by regular mail. The only thing Mr. Fusco had to do was flip the things over and endorse them in his capacity as administrator and chief executive officer. He had stacks of deposit slips and envelopes which helped ensure that the money went where it was supposed to go. Over twenty million laundered dollars passed through Mr. Fusco's hands every year. The Judge and Butch split 10% off the top as their share. The Patriarcas took 20%.

For his part, Al Fusco received about $400,000.00 in hospital salary and benefits. Local subordinates performed all the actual administrative duties within the small hospital. Not bad work if you can get it.

The trouble was that Al was unhappy. He wanted to be a big shot, a flashy, urban Mafiosi modeled after cinematic characters. But, that sort of attention-grabbing lifestyle was counterproductive to a career as a hospital administrator/banker, particularly the type of banker whose every transaction is illegal and whose clients are some of the most dangerous and powerful criminals on earth.

Fusco had run afoul of the Patriarca leadership in New York because of his absurd behavior. In Patrick County we would say that the boy was" smart enough", but he didn't have a lick of common sense. He spent money faster than he could earn it on exotic food, fine wine and "that" certain type of woman attracted to exotic food, fine wine and cash. He even had affairs with the wives of other family members. The usual punishment would have been a bullet in the back of the head and disposal in the East River but, Al was well-liked, smart and had potential. Also, "The Family" had a sizable investment in his education so they banished him to a pie job in Patrick County.

For Al, this was punishment, severe punishment. He was prudent enough to play the part and do the job, but in his heart, he regarded himself far superior to these "illiterate, dumbass, redneck hillbilly morons" by whom he imagined himself to be surrounded. He considered the Judge to be the smartest guy in the County and yet thought of him as a "stupid old ugly son of a bitch." In Butch Russell he saw someone with so few scruples that he could possibly do business with him. From the start he cultivated old Butch, an easy task since Butch regarded Fusco as the "cool kid" in school and was eager to be his friend and sidekick.

In Patrick County in the 1980's, there were no clubs, no bars, no theaters, no gyms, and only three restaurants in Stuart: The Virginian Motel dining room, a Dairy Queen and Texas Pizza. At dark, most folks just went home. A gathering of people at night typically meant somebody died and there was a wake. Yet, hidden away from the general public, there were small parties going on in the basements of fine houses on Sunset Drive among the few wealthy professionals. The older set got together and drank hard liquor while the under 40 group drank beer, smoked weed and sometimes used powder cocaine. Mr. Fusco wasn't invited. He couldn't fully be trusted. He didn't grow up here. Besides, he was the Judge's" Boy" and no one wanted to say something in an unguarded moment at a party that might get back to the Judge, something to which the Judge might take offense. No one wanted to offend the Judge, no matter who they were.

Bored, Mr. Fusco hated his new situation except for one thing; the women. Patrick County was well-blessed with singularly beautiful women, many of whom worked at the hospital. Al Fusco, the Adonis, the Greek god, the gift to all women, the fox who now found himself in the henhouse, never missed a chance to grope or paw the locals. Most were disgusted by his unwanted attentions and he was slapped and cursed quite often. At times one of these victims would complain to a boyfriend, husband, father or brother who then might storm the hospital loudly wanting to "kill that creepy son of a bitch" but there was never a formal complaint much less any discipline of the creepy son of a bitch because the victims desperately needed their jobs at the hospital and Mr. Fusco was, after all, the "Judge's Boy." None of these minor setbacks caused Al to change tactics. He just thought these women were too dumb to realize what he was offering and if he kept trying, sooner or later he would find one that would play along. Sooner or later, he'd find a woman who'd appreciate him for what a true gift to women he was. There had to be at least a few such women even in this backwoods outpost.

Mrs. Sylvia Baker had been an accountant in the hospital finance department for fifteen years. Born and bred in the county, she married her first and only boyfriend Clarence Baker. They had been married for twenty-five years. He was a midlevel manager in a textile plant. There were no children. The couple shared a comfortable life in a nice brick home. They drove new cars. Her principal interest apart from her work was her church. Every week was the same. She got up, fixed a nice breakfast, went to work, came home, fixed a nice supper, watched television with Clarence until 10:00 p.m. and then went to bed. She and Clarence slept in different bedrooms and except for per functional hugs and pecks on the cheek, she had not touched her husband in years. On Wednesday nights, they went to church. On Saturdays she went shopping in the morning and worked in the yard or the house in the afternoon. On Sundays, Sylvia went to church and then she and Clarence would eat lunch at The Virginian and then go home and take separate naps. Every year, on Fourth of July week, the couple went to Myrtle Beach where they lived pretty much as they did at home except that work was replaced with laying on the beach. At 43, she was attractive enough. She dressed in a very conservative mode. Her hairstyle was straight out of the 1950's (she went to "Carol's Clips" every other Monday). The thing was that Mrs. Sylvia Baker was sensual in -spite- of herself. Her calves were well-curved. Her hips round and firm. Her waist was narrow, her breasts large for her body size. Her green eyes were wide and inviting. She would have hated to hear that, but they were "bedroom eyes," "Come hither eyes."

Sylvia watched a lot of television, went to a lot of movies in Martinsville, and read a lot of romance novels and grocery store tabloids but she longed for something more in her own life. Excitement, perhaps. Change. Thrills. Something not so much the same. Every day was the same, every week was the same every year was the same. She was over forty. She looked down the road and saw old age followed by death. Outwardly, Sylvia Baker seemed content enough, but her life was slipping into deadly sameness when Alphonse Fusco came along.

From the first time she saw the new administrator, she felt a strong physical attraction which surprised and embarrassed her. She had never seen such a handsome man. As the new administrator, he came into her small office, sat on her desk and engaged in small talk to get to know her, so to speak. Sylvia became giddy. Fusco's exotic looks, friendly personality and easy smile carried her away to places she had never been. When he left, he squeezed her hand and she squeezed back. Over the next few days, every time she saw him, she smiled broadly, he smiled back. When they discussed some minor financial issue, he would gently caress the small of her back, sending chills up her spine that made her scalp tingle.

One afternoon Sylvia was in the small kitchen adjacent to the break room. Suddenly Mr. Fusco came in, locked the door and without saying a word embraced her and kissed her neck. Sylvia began breathing quickly and loudly, panting in fact. "Why, umm, Mr. Fusco…" Then she noticed that one of his hands was cupping her breast. She sucked in a sharp breath of air and "No… no…I really…I can't…I'm …" but now he had both hands around her waist and had sat her on the counter, pushing the coffee pot back with his hand. He began kissing her on the mouth. His eyes were closed but Sylvia kept her eyes open and continued to protest but it was impossible to speak with a mouth full of Fusco. Her dress was pushed up on her legs and her large white panties with the little flowers on them were pushed to the side and he was touching her, well…there! Sylvia thought she would faint. Nobody had ever touched her like that and then… they were making love! They were making love standing up with their clothes on! Sweet, Sweet Jesus! She didn't know people actually did things like that! It was all over in a minute. In addition to "Greek God" and "Adonis" Al Fusco had also been referred to in some circles in New York as "Rabbit." He kissed her on the cheek, pulled up his zipper and quickly left the room.

As he left, he said, "Thanks, Susan, I'll…uh…I'll see you later." He left poor Sylvia in a state of shock, sitting on the counter.

The first thing poor Sylvia did was to jump off the counter and relock the kitchenette door. Then she began to cry. After a while, she regained her composure a bit, washed her face and rearranged her clothes. She had just been raped by her boss next to the coffee pot but as her nerves settled, outrage was not the emotion Sylvia experienced. Sylvia Baker had a lover! Not just any lover, the best looking man she'd ever seen, and a rich man at that! She could leave Clarence and move in with Mr. Fusco. They would be married! Her friends would be amazed. Church would be a thing of her past after she dumped Clarence. Maybe she would go to church with Mr. Fusco? He looked like a Presbyterian to Sylvia. She could quit work and shop all day. Really shop. Not just at the grocery store. Mrs. Sylvia Fusco! She smiled as she thought about it. Even after rearranging herself Sylvia thought that anybody seeing her could tell what had happened, she fled the hospital, went straight home and took a long hot bath.

The trouble was that while Mr. Fusco wanted sex with women, he didn't like women. His love of himself left little room for the love of anyone else. He had rarely been with a given woman more than once. You might say he was a one trick pony or rabbit as the case might be. He had no desire for conversation nor cuddling with a woman. He spent his spare time exercising to polish his body appearance and pampered himself with designer men's products. If he thought about "Susan What's –Her-Name" down in finance at all, it was to hope she wouldn't rat him out to some annoying husband or to some dumb cop. Even if she did, he'd just deny everything. He could say she was crazy! She could be fired. It'd be OK. The Judge could handle it. Maybe he ought to fire her anyway? Besides, he was preoccupied with his true passion: making a lot of money without working for it.

One cold, miserable night in March, Al Fusco invited Butch Russell to his lavish office in the small hospital after one of the infrequent hospital board meetings. The two men puffed on large expensive cigars and sipped old expensive whiskey. They talked about how stupid the hospital board members were and how clever the Judge was. Butch held his nose and did a passing imitation of the old Judge. "You boys just do what I tell 'ya and I'll make you rich. Damn rich." It was a phrase the Judge spoke often because of potential drug residues, milk should not be used for human consumption for forty- eight hours after the last dose of medicine, nor should the animal be slaughtered for human consumption for thirty- five days. I scrawled "Thank you" across the bottom of the paper and signed it.

In the cold black night, the comfortable brick farmhouse of Ellis Ryder looked cozy and downright inviting. I squished around to the back door hoping that if I took off my boots, I might be invited in. Hell, I'd have stripped off buck naked just to sit by a warm stove for a few minutes at that point.

I knocked on the door several times and eventually heard stirring around in the quiet house. I could see lights coming on one by one showing the progress being made toward the back door. After a clattering of bolts and door chains, the large door creaked open and Ellis appeared. He certainly didn't look like the walking mud ball he had been when I last saw him. He was wrapped in a huge thick faded red robe and his remaining white hair stood straight up. His skin was red and appeared well-scrubbed. He had that glow you see in an old dog after giving it a good bath.

Instead of inviting me in, Ellis shuffled out on the small cold porch and closed the door behind him. He glanced at me and his overall appearance was grim. I was all set to deliver the happy news about the cow and calf, get my money and head home to my own personal clean up, but before I could say anything, Ellis began to speak. "I don't want her to hear this. You may have heard that my wife Edna has got the cancer. She's eaten up with it. We been fightin' it for two years now and it ain't done no good. She don't have much time left. It's a terrible thing. I...I shouldn't have called you over here tonight. I knew I couldn't pay 'ya, Doc. We got insurance where I work but I still owe over twenty-thousand dollars. May as well be a million. The hospital up here has garnished my paycheck. They only left us a hundred a week to live on and...well...I...worked my whole life..." Now Ellis became choked up and the tears were filling his eyes. He shook his head and looked down for a few seconds as he composed himself. "If it weren't for our grown kids...we'd uh...we'd a lost everything." Now he looked up at me for the first time. "I'm gonna pay you. Every cent if it's the last thing I do." He shook my hand and went back in the house, locking the door. He never asked about the cow and calf.

I went home and took a hot shower. I was drinking a cup of coffee when the tones went off. A sixty-seven-year-old woman was having chest pains and difficulty breathing on the mile straight. I signed on, got dressed and went back out into the cold night.

Meanwhile, in the lavish office of the hospital administrator, Butch and Al were finishing up their expensive whiskey and their expensive cigars. Butch leaned in toward Al and said quietly as if he thought an eavesdropper might hear him, "How much do you figure we'll make on this deal?"

Al shook his head and looked pensive. "It's really difficult to come up with exact numbers. I've done a lot of work on it and I did arrive at a conservative estimate. There's overhead I may have underestimated and such but we're probably looking at around $50,000.00."

"In a year?"

"No. Per month"

"To split between just us?"

"No. Each."

Butch was stunned. He also was no longer having trouble staying awake. "I'll get right to work on those contracts." There was a long pause during which neither man spoke, and Butch stared at a point on the floor. "Well, it's late and I'd better go." They shook hands and with that handshake the foxes, entrusted to protect it, agreed to loot the henhouse. On his way home Butch saw the flashing red lights of the JEB Stuart ambulance, but he didn't particularly care.

Al Fusco was now alone in his magnificent office; the office the hospital paid for at the Judge's orders. The office designed by an interior decorator from New York City, built by a construction firm from Atlanta, furnished by a company in High Point and decorated with carpets, drapes and curios from all around the world. The whiskey and the cigar had left him with a warm fuzzy feeling, he took a moment to congratulate himself. He had been sent to "Hillbilly World" as a punishment, but he, Alphonse G. Fusco, was clever enough to take advantage of any situation. He was surrounded by morons. It was absurdly easy. If the Judge and Butch were the smartest guys in the room, then the room was filled with idiots and those two were the chief imbeciles. Al laughed aloud at the image. He wasn't in New York or Boston or Chicago. He wasn't engaged in the typical

We had given up any pretense of keeping Old Midnight the wonder dog in sight. He would vanish into the blizzard and we would hear his barking become faint, then he would charge out of the snow racing past us and into the dark in another direction. I wondered what this dog would do if he actually found the missing hunter. I decided he might race past him ignoring our victim completely, or the stupid dog might just eat the lost hunter. I had no confidence in this dog at all. The three of us on two legs had long stopped that foolishness of running through the snow and were now trudging, taking high steps and silently making progress to nowhere. After what seemed to be hours, the wind began to lay, and the snow fell softly, quietly. The blizzard had (for the most part) abated.

My thoughts turned to Napoleon's epic retreat from Moscow. He lost most of his *Grande Armee,* many due to freezing. I remembered the paintings I had seen of the poor wretches frozen in agony. Then I thought how that march had stretched over hundreds of miles with mounted Cossacks attacking at every opportunity. If we went a few miles in any direction, we would go from nowhere to somewhere! I reasoned that almost no matter what else might happen I was unlikely to freeze to death and of all the things I had to worry about, mounted Cossacks wasn't one of them. I was still miserable, but somewhat comforted by the thought that I wasn't as bad off as the French soldiers in the long ago retreat from Moscow.

Then, way off in the distance, I saw a small pinpoint of light. At first, I wasn't even sure it was real, but as I stared at it I became convinced that whatever that light was, it was where I wanted to be. I stuck my hand out and Earl walked into it. He had been plodding along dumbly as if he were a ghost. A weird frozen ghost. I pointed to the tiny light. "Look!" I yelled, "Let's go over there!" and the two of us started out for the elusive small light. "Hey, E.G.!" I shouted over my shoulder, "We're leaving! Bye!"

"Wait a minute, Men, we need to follow the dog!" shouted back the Trooper.

"Fuck that stupid ass dog!" I don't know if Trasker heard me or not as by that time we were both powering through the snow as if we were Russian soldiers surrounding Stalingrad. Was it a house? Had we circled back to the fire and the ambulance? Well, no. Incredibly, it was our lost hunter. An experienced woodsman, he wasn't sure where he was when it began to snow and it was getting dark so rather than wander about making things worse, he had made a lean-to of pine boughs and started a fire. He figured that in the morning, he'd just get oriented and walk home. He sure didn't expect a rescue party to show up. 'Course Earl, and I were in need of rescue more than anybody. We were both snow-covered and panting. Skinny little Earl was dancing around. His skin was a new shade of pale and his teeth were chattering.

"Hey, Fellas. Have some coffee. What are you guys doing out this time of night?" asked the lost hunter, an old friend of mine.

"Thanks" I said as I grabbed the hot metal cup of brown fluid that passed for coffee. "We're out looking for you."

"Well, you found me. Now what?"

To be honest about it, I really hadn't given much thought to that part of the exercise. I assumed we'd just figure it out. I had my walkie-talkie, but it wasn't working. I'd had trouble with the battery holding a charge, or maybe the snow had shorted it out. Whatever the case, it looked like the three of us were on our own. Earl had left his radio at home. Eventually, a subdued E. G. Trasker arrived. His radio wasn't working either. It occurred to me that this was a singularly incompetent search and rescue operation. I was also sure that we shared the same thought: "Now what?"

"We'll have to pile up to share body heat and sleep through the night. We'll take turns staying awake to keep the fire going and we'll set out at first light." said Trasker quietly. To me, that was a grim plan and as I imagined, it I became more miserable.

As the four of us sat staring morosely into the small fire, we suddenly heard motor noises and then the place was flooded with bright lights. It was the ambulance! We didn't realize it in the dark, but by sheer luck our hunter had pitched his camp a few feet from a public road! Anthony Price, after long arguing with Walter, had decided to take the four-wheel drive ambulance and check the public roads for us, reasoning that we would most likely come out on a road.

Anthony nearly ran over me as I jumped out in front of the unit wildly waving my arms. As drowning survivors of a shipwreck clamber onto a raft so we all jumped into the back of the ambulance. There are no words to describe that first feeling of warmth, real warmth. As we thawed out, we began laughing and reliving our experience. All except the Trooper. I don't think he laughed very much.

Since the "whole body lift" hadn't worked, Larry and Rusty next tried to pull up on the involved leg, but as soon as they touched Donnie's thigh he yelled, "God you're killing me! You're killing me, goddammit! Just shoot me! If you're gonna kill me just shoot me and get it over with!"

Larry and Rusty retreated a bit and put their heads together. "Maybe we should call the fire Department and get 'em to cut a big hole in the floor so we can get down and splint the leg where it is." offered Larry.

At this point the drunken crowd went wild. Heaping abuse on the volunteers and threatening physical violence. Ed Quinn had been standing largely unnoticed next to the cot watching the goings-on with folded arms and growing disgust.

A particularly drunk loud older woman got in Ed's face and screamed like a Harpy, "Don't just stand there, asshole! Help the man! Can't you see he's sufferin'? For God's sake!"

Ed Quinn didn't say a word. He uncrossed his arms and walked slowly and deliberately over to the suffering Donnie Cox and got down on his hands and knees. The sight of such a big man moving into position to help caused an expectant hush to fall over the crowd. Even Donnie became quiet. Ed picked up a flashlight and shined it into the hole, placing his head against Donnie's entrapped leg.

Ed started speaking slowly and softly. It was the only sound in the now-still room. "Don't worry, Donnie. I ain't gonna touch you. I just want to look. Yeah. Yeah. I can see your thigh. Looks all right. I can see your knee that looks fine too...so does your shin bone. Doesn't seem broken to me. Ankle looks good. I can see your foot. Still has your shoe on... Whoowee, Look at the size of that rattlesnake!"

Donnie Cox pulled his leg out of the hole like a rocket, striking Ed Quinn on his cheek with his knee. Once free of the hole, Donnie danced around the room as if he were Mr. Bojangles. Ed struggled to his feet rubbing the bruise on his cheek. He handed his clipboard to Donnie. "Here, Donnie, sign this where it says, 'Refused transport' so we can go home."

Back in the ambulance, Rusty asked Ed, "It's the middle of winter, Ed. Ain't no rattlesnakes out this time of year are there?"

"Nope." said Ed Quinn packing his mouth with chewing tobacco, "Too cold for 'em."

Larry Cane picked up the microphone as Ed put the ambulance into motion. "JEB 300 to Patrick. 10-8 back to station."

"10-4 300."

"You will see what people do to one another; you'll see wives with their faces battered by their husbands, you will see children with broken limbs and scalded skin. You will see knifings, slashings and the terrible things a bullet can do to a body. It's nothing like the movies."

I walked into a small house one night to find a distraught woman seated on a couch and holding her badly damaged nose. "Who did this to you, and where is he?" I asked. Most family violence comes from within the family itself.

"He's in the bathroom," she said pointing, "and he's got a gun, but don't worry, he's gonna shoot himself."

That's just great. The scene wasn't safe as long as an armed man, whatever his intention, was just down the hall. The Sheriff Drew Watson brand of law enforcement was notoriously slow to respond, especially to a violent incident so we were on our own. Carefully, I crept down the hall toward the closed bathroom door. I gently knocked on the door.

"Hey, uh, we need to …uh…work on your wife here and…uh…I can't let my crew come in the house if you're in here with a gun. I wonder if you could hand me the gun." My crew, consisting of Larry Cane and Jarrell Price were already in the house and attempting to tend to the wife, who was actively refusing all treatment.

"That you, Doc?" came the reply from the other side of the closed door. "What are you doin' here? Is the dog sick?"

"No. Far as I know, the dog's fine. I'm runnin' with JEB these days and I really need you to hand me the gun."

"Nope. They'll send me back to jail and I ain't goin'. But don't worry, Doc, I'm gonna shoot myself and you guys won't have to mess with it. Just call the funeral home."

"Hey, look, don't do that." I replied, my mind racing, "If you do that, I'll have to fill out paperwork all night, and I need to get home as soon as I can and get some sleep. And…uh… your wife said she loves you and she ain't goin' to press charges or nothin'."

I heard him laugh and then he said, "You're lying. If you give her this gun, she'll shoot me herself." There was a long pause. I was holding my breath, halfway expecting to hear a gunshot. "Ah, shit, I'll come out." He did and he handed me an empty Roma Rocket .22 revolver. After that, we stood around the hallway talking about different things, like what a piece of junk a Roma Rocket is. Jarrell and Larry talked quietly with the wife, trying to calm her down. At one point she did in fact say that if we'd give her the gun, she'd shoot him herself. After a long while, two deputies showed up, and, well, yeah, took the husband to jail.

As we got back into the ambulance, Larry mimicked the man's voice, "...is the dog sick?" It seemed funny at the time.

Most people who say they want to kill themselves really don't. Almost every person that we saved from a suicide came around later to thank the volunteers; which makes the number of successful suicides even more tragic. People have no idea that the suicide rate is so high. Rarely are suicides reported as news items. In obituaries the euphemism used is "...died at the home." The phrase sounds so peaceful and conjures up images of a quiet, non-public death surrounded by friends and family; but too often, what the rescue squad finds is a body hanging by a rope the face contorted, swollen and black, or blood and brains sprayed on the walls and a gun on the floor, or a discolored corpse next to an empty bottle of pills. Then there are the fatal car accidents which seem suspiciously deliberate: the car on a straight road slams into a tree with no sign of braking or any attempt to avoid the impact.

One Sunday afternoon, a husband was drinking as his wife drove along the back roads, a typical Sunday afternoon activity for the couple. The car developed a flat tire and the wife pulled into the parking lot of a small country store. The drunken husband got out, inspected the flat tire and began to blame his wife. As he attempted to change the wheel, he became more and more enraged, first slapping the poor woman and then, for some awful reason, he began to savagely beat her with the tire iron. The store owner heard the screams and came out, firing a shotgun into the air. The husband fled leaving his unconscious wife on the ground.

When we arrived, the woman had regained consciousness, but her face was a mess and her injuries were obviously severe. Lucinda Gray was with me and she gently began cleaning the wounds with sterile gauze wet with sterile saline. Lucinda said very little but held the victim in her typical, intense gaze as she silently worked. Anthony Price was our driver. Lucinda and I gently packaged the victim, and when we were ready, Anthony and I carefully loaded her into the unit. She could barely talk. Lucinda was using suction to remove blood from her mouth as we headed to the hospital. "If I die" she said weakly, "make sure they put him in the electric chair." An understandable sentiment. However, during the long ambulance ride, her feelings changed. She wondered if the officers might hurt her husband when they caught him. She began to cry and said over and over that it was all her fault. As we neared the emergency room, she was asking herself what she was going to do without her man. She began begging God to bring her husband back to her.

Lucinda stared into the poor woman's frightened eyes. "No. Don't talk like that. You go to the law and try to get him locked up forever and then you divorce him or you get one of his guns and you shoot the son of a bitch right in the head and you don't stop until the gun is totally empty."

"What!?" said Anthony from up front. He jumped in the seat as if he'd had an electrical shock. "Don't be telling her that mess! Just shut up, Lucinda. We're almost at the hospital. What's wrong with you?"

It occurred to me that family violence may have played a part in shaping Lucinda into the somewhat strange woman she had become.

"I don't hate guns. Matter of fact, I make my living largely from selling guns, but when you see gunshot wounds, and the tremendous damages they do you start to think. Maybe there are too many guns. Maybe there are too many damn guns."

I did see gunshot wounds, but not as many as one would expect, considering how heavily armed the Patrick County population is and how short-tempered some of our citizens are. From what I could tell, knives and blunt objects were more often used as tools of assault than guns. If there was a shooting, usually the shooter would be there, holding the gun and warning us that if we revived the victim, he'd just shoot again. Whenever I see the damage a bullet does to perfectly good humans and animals the same thought crosses my mind: Damn guns.

Paul continued describing different violent scenes volunteers might encounter, but my mind was still wandering. A call came one night that "…a man was lying down in a cemetery." That sounded odd but conjured up images of a sick or drunk individual napping peacefully among the memorials. I happened to be driving nearby, so I went directly to the scene

ain't safe." Of course, Ed was right, all my training had been to pull back and wait for the scene to become safer, but then…I glanced at Rusty, he looked at me and we smiled, like two kids pulling off a really cool prank.

"I'm goin' in the rear window. You hand the stuff in to me." The stuff was already on the cot and we rolled it up to the rear bumper. Maggie was there organizing the lifesaving tools to be handed in to the car. Ed was there too, sighing and muttering that we were destined to become crispy critters. We were wading in gasoline. I folded myself through the window and in the dim light I saw the apparently lifeless body of a beautiful young lady lying on her right side across the front seat. My heart sank. Traumatic death is unimaginably tragic.

I began to follow my training. "A" for "Airway." She was not noticeably breathing and her efforts at breathing were a series of short jerks. As I checked her airway, I found out what was wrong: an entire tape cassette was filling her mouth impeding the free exchange of air. I removed the cassette, she gagged once and then began to breathe in a way that passed for normal. Rusty was right behind me in the rear seat handing me a non-rebreathing mask which was attached by tube to a small tank of oxygen. As I fitted the mask onto our recumbent patient it occurred to me that I was working in a closed space filled with a mixture of gasoline fumes and pure oxygen. Not a good time to get nervous and light up a cigarette. "B" is for "Breathing." With Fleetwood Mac out of her mouth and the high flow oxygen flowing, she seemed to be breathing acceptably. I used the stethoscope to quickly check out her chest. Equal sounds. No dead places or areas of resonance. "C" is for "Circulation." A quick check showed no major bleeding although she was probably in shock or heading that way. Her skin was cool and dry, her heart rate was rapid she was unconscious. "D" is for "Deformity." Her left thigh was shorter than it should have been and obviously swollen suggesting a fracture of the left femur or thigh bone, probably due to the steering column, which was itself bent. LOC is "Level of Consciousness." She was not awake, but she was responsive to painful stimuli.

We had already spent entirely too much time in this death trap. The gasoline fumes were so thick, I was getting a headache. 'Course a headache is preferable to being burned alive. Rusty and I feverishly applied an E-collar and a vest-like K.E.D. board. As we scrambled back out through the rear window, carrying the KED-Boarded, still unconscious girl with us, I was relieved to see the volunteer firemen, and hear the sound of the pumper truck diluting the volatile gas and washing it away. The firemen helped us carry the lucky girl to the backboard on the cot and move her to the ambulance which Ed had pulled a safe distance away. I gently cradled the broken left leg.

Once we were safely in the ambulance, Maggie began a more thorough examination while Rusty and I applied a Hare traction splint to the broken leg.

The femur or thigh bone is a massive bone surrounded by large, powerful muscles. If this bone becomes fractured, the bone ends typically override each other shortening the thigh and causing those powerful leg muscles to ball up and spasm. The effect is extremely painful. Also, if the sharp ends of broken bone flail around in the thigh during transport, muscle can be damaged. Nerves and blood vessels can also be lacerated. If the huge femoral artery becomes cut, it is usually a "game over" situation and the patient rapidly bleeds to death. One end of the Hare traction device attaches to the hip and upper femur. The other end is attached to the foot. Using an adjustable frame and a ratcheted crank, the femur is gently straightened lining up the bone ends and arresting the painful spasm of the large leg muscles. The bone ends are also immobilized, minimizing additional trauma during transport. It's a handy little machine and takes only a minute or two to apply.

As we headed for the hospital, I began intravenous fluids into her arms. Maggie checked the blood pressure and pulse while Rusty requested helicopter transport. Ed drove smoothly to the emergency room.

Several months later, I saw our patient at the pizza place. She was using a cane, but otherwise appeared none the worse for wear. She didn't recognize me. There was no reason for her to. If you're looking for recognition and gratitude, the volunteer rescue squad isn't the place.

"Your patients in their pain, their anger, their emotional distress may say and do things that severely try your patience, but don't let it get to you. You're not the average guy on the street. You are there to help. Not to judge and certainly not to punish."

Another time, teenager had taken (borrowed) her daddy's car without permission and had evidently "borrowed" some of his whiskey to go along with it. Bad plan. Shortly after starting this little adventure, she hit a tree and broke her femur. She told us she was twenty-two and old enough to refuse treatment, which she did. Some would-be good Samaritans had helped her out of the car, she was seated on the grass next to the wrecked car screaming obscenities about the pain, the stupid car and the stupid tree. Jarrell Price knew her and convinced her to let us apply a Hare traction splint and transport her to the hospital. He told her that if she didn't get her leg fixed it would rot off. She refused to be otherwise packaged. As Jarrell put on the Hare device, she called him every name anyone ever thought of and used obscenities in creative combinations I had never heard before (and I grew up in the 60's). I had served in the Army and thought I had heard all the cussing there was, but this girl proved me wrong.

"Jarrell, you goddam motherfucking shitbag Negro, stop hurting my son-of-a-bitching stupid ass leg!" as she grabbed the hair on Jarrell's head and began violently shaking it. "Oh fuck, fuck, fuck, fuck, fuck your hairy ass black hide!"

Jarrell worked calmly and patiently, gently straightening the deformed leg. Then there was an audible "pop". Our victim stopped shaking Jarrell's head and gave a huge sigh. The screaming stopped. "Lord God, it quit hurting! How'd you do that?" She not only quit screaming, but now she was smiling. "Jarrell, you're a sweetheart! Come here. I want to give you a great big kiss. You're really cute. Are you going with anyone?"

We loaded her carefully into the ambulance and sped off to the hospital. Jarrell was a true professional throughout the whole ordeal. I couldn't tell the bigger victim; the teenager with a broken leg or Jarrell.

"When you come to realize how much mayhem on our roads is directly attributable to drunk driving you may come to think like I do, damn alcohol."

On a bright, beautiful Sunday morning a large sedan ran off a straight road, up an embankment, flipped upside down and slid on its roof down the highway. Again, access to the interior was greatly limited. On our arrival, a very well-dressed but obviously drunk woman was standing in the road screaming "My Baby! My Baby! Lord Jesus my Baby's in that car!" The hair on my head stood up. Without a second's delay I dived into the wreckage to save the baby; but on my way in, I encountered an older man, also well-dressed, also drunk, picking his way out. After grandpa got out and stood up, the woman hugged him, covered him with kisses and cried,

"Oh Baby! Oh, my Baby! I thought I'd never see you again!" Larry Cane laughed so hard he had trouble catching his breath. He kept pointing at me and saying that I should have seen the expression on my face. Anyway, the two lovers signed a release, refused treatment and left with their friends before the law showed up, avoiding potentially embarrassing sobriety tests.

In response to anger over drunk-driving, legislators passed tougher and tougher drunk-driving laws with severe penalties including permanent loss of driving privileges, high fines and significant jail sentences. I think these laws should have been collectively titled "The Lawyer Relief Acts." The severe penalties made it worthwhile to spend any amount of money and go to any lengths to avoid a drunk-driving conviction, especially in the case of multiple offenders.

One rainy summer Saturday afternoon, I rolled the ambulance to an overturned vehicle call. A new pickup truck was "wheels-up" on the side of the road with steam hissing from the engine compartment. When I arrived, there was a prominent real estate agent wearing a muddy shirt and staggering around the side of the road. He was obviously intoxicated, and there was, as they say, the strong smell of alcohol. He told me that a large brown dog had run out in front of him and in his efforts to avoid the poor animal, he had lost control and overturned. "You would've done the same thing, right, Doc? You and me, why we'd gladly wreck a car to avoid hurtin' some dog? Am I right?" His speech was thick and slurred.

Walter Mayhew, never one to miss a chance to ingratiate himself to someone he considered rich and important, was comforting the man and advising him to run away before the cops showed up. The drunk looked at Walter open-mouthed, and dumbfounded, running anywhere was not an option. The trooper showed up and after checking found our "dog saver" had three previous convictions for DUI dating back to when he was 18 years old. He flunked the field sobriety test in a big way. He not only couldn't walk a straight- line, he couldn't even stand on it. He kept staggering off to one side or the other. When asked to touch his finger to his nose, he simply fell down with his foot sticking up in the air. He blew a 4.0 which means you or I would have been comatose had we consumed that much alcohol. As he had refused treatment and transport, he was placed in the back seat of the patrol car and taken to jail. There were several empty whiskey bottles in the truck. "That drunk bastard" said Anthony

old daughter, returned to Patrick County. A rebellious teenager had left but a grown woman/mother returned.

Melody's parents had racial attitudes common during that time and in that place, but the little half-breed girl was so beautiful and personable that, well, love overrode all other considerations. The parents welcomed back their prodigal daughter and doted over their exceptional grandchild. Melody mended her relationship with her mother and the conflicts of the past stayed in the past. The three adults dedicated themselves to making Nedra's childhood as wonderful and happy as it could possibly be.

Nedra LaPeltier grew up to become the most beautiful girl enrolled at Patrick County High School. Practically every boy therein considered violating his parent's admonitions against dating black girls to be with her. The boy who won the prize was Emory Ward Russell, known as Ward to his friends, the namesake and direct descendent of the carpet bagger who came to Patrick County after the Civil War in a wagon filled with dry goods and gold bars. His grandfather was Fleet Taylor, the bootlegger, car salesman and "Legend of NASCAR." His mother was Joan Taylor Russell. His father was none other than William Henry Harrison Russell, known as "Butch", the Commonwealth's Attorney for Patrick County, Chairman of the hospital board of trustees, close associate to the Judge and partner of Al Fusco. When just seventeen years old and entering her senior year of high school, Nedra discovered that she was pregnant. She became Mrs. E. Ward Russell shortly thereafter.

Ward Russell was a fine-looking specimen and considered a good catch around the County if for no other reason than the prominence and wealth of his family. He wasn't perfect. He was the youngest of three children and as the "baby" was hopelessly spoiled by his mother. He was lazy to a fault and why not? He had won the lottery at birth. He had it made. He didn't need to work. He didn't need to worry. He was born with a silver spoon and he intended to eat off it his entire life.

He started using cigarettes in grade school, was drinking heavily by tenth grade and was using drugs shortly thereafter. He developed a true love for marijuana, smoking prodigious amounts of the stuff. As a boyfriend in high school he was a lot of fun. He was a thrill ride. Nedra enjoyed the attention she got from the other high school girls as "the prize" who got "the catch." She never really decided if she loved Ward or not.

She did like him, yet as a husband to Nedra and a father to their daughter Druisilla, he left much to be desired.

The new family moved in with the Russell parents into their rambling mansion. In fact, they moved into Ward's childhood room. Even in 1979, the obviously mixed racial heritage of Nedra was hardly welcome. Joan was cold and unfriendly toward her new daughter-in-law making no attempt to mask her disappointment with Ward's choice. Butch's widowed mother Eleanor, who lived in the mansion rarely referred to Nedra by her name but rather as "that Niggra what married Ward."

Butch looked past Nedra's racial background. He saw what most men did: a very attractive, sexy, young girl. Butch would literally salivate over her, but then you see, Butch was a pervert. He paid Monk Fisher to give money to local young couples and then video them having sex at the local Motel. Butch was a special brand of pervert. He didn't want to see anonymous pornography. No. He wanted to see the girl who served him his pizza at Texas Restaurant, the girl who checked him out at the Supermarket and that cute clerk down at the convenience store. He watched the videos over and over, pleasuring himself from the sexual intimacies of Patrick County children. Perverted sexual pornography was as addictive to Butch Russell as heroin.

While the Russell's begrudgingly provided room and board, they never offered Nedra or Drusilla any direct cash support. After drugs and whiskey, Ward had little left of his own weekly allowance to contribute to his small family. If Nedra wanted money, she would have to work for it. So she got a job as a checker at the Piggly Wiggly Supermarket.

The maid took care of Druisilla while Nedra worked and Ward embarked on a career of marijuana and whiskey. It was far from a happy home. Ward also made it his business to fuck as many of the local whores as would hold still, which included most of them. Soon Nedra and Druisilla moved into the room across the hall. She and Ward avoided each other. Days and sometimes weeks would pass without speaking to or seeing each other, even though they were married and lived in the same house. Whenever they did interact, it usually developed into a fight and the fights became more and more physically violent. Nedra was no pushover and she gave as good as she got but she frequently wore the bruises, cuts and scars of a battered wife. Nedra realized there would be no one to rescue her. No one, not her family, not the law, not any of her many friends would dare go up against the powerful Russell family.

The breaking point came one evening when Nedra came home after a long day at work to hear the sounds of sex coming from the room across the hall. She burst into Ward's room expecting to find him fucking some slut. Instead Ward was all alone in the darkened room, watching an old black and white pornographic video on the VCR. (Like Father like Son.) He was buck naked and high as a kite (which wasn't all that unusual) but this time he had shaved off all his hair. All of it. To the very last sprig of hair over his entire body.

"What the hell is wrong with you?" she demanded.

"Oh… Uh… yeah… see… I saw on the news that they got… uh… some kind of way of seeing if you… uh… you know…finding out if you use dope and all by checking your hair so… uh… you know… I… like shaved all that shit off." he said as he took a long pull on a joint. The marijuana smoke was thick in the air and the room reeked of alcohol, urine, sweat and smoke. Nedra was disgusted. She lost her temper.

"That's it! Fuck this! Fuck you! It's over you bastard! Dru and I are leaving, you can hang around here shaving your balls all you want, but you're doing it without me! God damn your crazy ass I've tried, Lord knows I have, but this tears it! I am out of here! DO YOU HEAR ME? I'm leaving you! I'm leaving you now! Forever!"

Ward made no response. He stared at his wife dumbly with the expression of a cow that has just been shot in the head. He took another long toke on the joint that made a little flame appear at the end of the rolled paper.

Nedra was past mad. She slammed the door, gathered up her two-year-old daughter from the maid, and went downstairs. As she passed the kitchen, she saw Mrs. Joan Russell, old Mrs. Eleanor Russell and the black cook all fixing supper. Nedra stopped in the kitchen doorway and addressed the group. "He's crazy! Do you people know that? He is crazy and Dru and I are leaving!" she screamed.

The two Mrs. Russell's looked at Nedra with expressions of open-mouthed shock on their faces, not at the news that Ward was crazy, but shock that his wife (a mulatto at that) would dare to talk to them in that tone of voice. Joan Russell answered quietly, "Now Dear, the best thing we can do is to pray over it. Put it in God's hands and hope that Jesus will touch his heart and heal him."

"*Jesus? Jesus!* You're all *crazy*! All of you! Fuck you all!" and with that she left the Russell mansion forever going home to her grandparents and her mother taking nothing more than her child and the clothes on her back.

The divorce was quick and handled out of court. Drusilla's paternity was called into question. Nedra was branded "a faithless spouse with sexually promiscuous tendencies" and neither alimony nor child support was awarded. Well, at least it was over. Nedra petitioned the court to change their names from Russell to LaPeltier. The petition was granted quickly.

While some women with Nedra's looks and in Nedra's situation would have just gone husband hunting and hooked some guy to support the young mother and her child; Nedra was her daddy's daughter. She had Eddy LaPeltier's independence, his strength, his determination and his daring. Nedra was going to do it on her own. She wasn't sure she ever wanted another man in her life but if one came along it would be on her terms: not from desperation nor accident but by choice. Her choice. And if there was to be another guy, he damn sure better make her happy.

She kept her job at the Piggly Wiggly. As she worked, she looked over at Ol' Liz working away at the next register. Liz had been a checker at the Piggly Wiggly for 32 years. She wasn't making much more than Nedra. That life may have suited Ol' Liz, but Nedra was her daddy's daughter. She wanted more. She knew there were other horizons and she had a compelling desire to see them. She was young, beautiful and smart. Piggly Wiggly would not be her final destination on the road of life if she could help it.

For a young woman without family wealth, the highest paying job in this area was that of a Registered Nurse; and actually in the back of her mind, Nedra had often thought about it as a career.

She was very young at the time, yet she remembered going to a hospital with her mother that horrible night her Daddy drowned. She could not comprehend what was happening, of course, but a beautiful nurse in a white dress had comforted and hugged her. She was so gentle, so kind, and she smelled clean and sweet. As tragic as the night had been, that nurse had been a life-long warm memory for Nedra. So, she would be a nurse. A nurse and cavorting with a pole. It breeds resentment among the performers. Resentment and contempt for their audience and in some cases all men. A certain camaraderie develops backstage among the dancers and it's not surprising that some turn to other women for affection and love. The ladies themselves are in most instances "decent" and their motives are decent, often trying to support and educate children so that their daughters may be spared the necessity of this path to survival.

These dancers are typically neither sluts nor prostitutes. They are victims of circumstance. Very few strip naked for pleasure. It is exploitation with the unfair exercise of power by the powerful over the less so. It's not that exotic dancers are overpaid, not at all. The problem is that our society so poorly rewards women for their other valuable contributions. That failure to achieve financial security in conventional occupations may lead to exotic dancing or worse.

The men, sitting in the dark, sipping the over-priced watered-down drinks (while successful by their measurements) are usually failed personalities at some level. They snicker and wink at each other. As if schoolboys sharing dirty jokes they do not fully understand. Individually, they are usually failures at interactions with the women in their lives. As a group, they become empowered. They are immature bullies who can compel young women to do their collective bidding.

A regular participant in this group was Butch Russell. He drove down to **The Fox Pen** at least once a week to sit in the dark and ogle the show. As was the case with most of the clientele, Butch hoped that few would recognize him in such a distant venue, after all it's an embarrassing habit for a Common Wealth's Attorney to have. He was usually too drunk to safely drive home on the after-midnight return trips but Butch had been driving home under the influence for so many years that he wasn't concerned about the risk.

Then one night, the announcer introduced "Victoria, The African Queen." Butch nearly choked on his over-priced watered- down drink when he saw his ex-daughter-in-law enter the spotlight.

Nedra wore very high-heeled black shoes, white fishnet stockings held up by fancy red garters, a sequined T-back, dangling earrings, gold bangles on both wrists and a large gold necklace. She began dancing to Bobbi Gentry's *Fancy*. Her performance was so beautiful and fluid that it rose above mere prurience to the level of art. It was in some ways the fulfillment of Butch's wildest dreams.

Nedra began stripping while attending nursing school. One of her fellow students suggested it as a way to make ends meet. At first, Nedra took it as a joke then one Saturday night she went with her classmate to a club in Greensboro. She was hired on the spot, and the next weekend she did her first show. It was uncomfortable, but not as bad as she thought it might be and the money was surprisingly good. Nedra did have natural talents for this type of work. For one, she was as beautiful naked as she was with her clothes on. For another, she was athletic and flexible; she could perform well without physical exhaustion. She became a regular dancer on weekends in this club. The place was old and less than clean with a rowdy obnoxious crowd. Some of the other dancers suggested she try out for **The Fox Pen.** She met with Dewey and his current girlfriend in his office. After some small talk and introductions, Dewey asked her to take off all her clothes and turn around a few times. He was looking for any hesitancy or shyness. As a horse breeder might examine a prospective mare to add to his stable, Dewey had her perform some moves. She must have passed his test, for he handed her a copy of the club rules and asked her which nights she would work. Nedra picked Friday and Saturday nights. She then dressed and drove back to Patrick County in time for her nursing classes. Later, after graduation and employed at the Patrick County hospital, she requested and was granted first shift hours on Fridays.

Nedra was astonished by the money she made. Dewey, unlike most club owners, paid his performers a fairly- decent wage. In addition to their tips (in some clubs, the girls worked only for the tips.) Nedra was soon making more money in two nights stripping than she made nursing full time the other days of the week. She religiously put the extra money away for Druisilla. As the job entailed a lot of driving, she did buy herself a nice used BMW 733i. It was black with a black leather interior. No one was allowed to eat in that car. She kept her other old car to drive around locally and eat in.

Stripping wasn't that bad, and it was a financial bonanza. Nevertheless, had she known Butch Russell was in the audience, she would have quit immediately.

a nurse and… a stripper. It served her well. She knew that a confrontational approach with Butch wouldn't work and may be dangerous. Instead, she adopted a flattering, almost fawning attitude toward him at their meetings.

She paid Dewey extra so that the sessions would last over an hour if need be. When Dewey asked her what was going on, she said that this guy was really confused, and that he was using her as his shrink. If she were to cut him off, the poor man might commit suicide and she had enough on her conscience already. Nedra was a basically honest person, but when need be, she was an accomplished liar. Dewey assented to the arrangement but said it might be better if they met in a motel room outside of business hours. Of course, there was no way for any reason that Nedra would go into a motel room with Butch Russell.

"Butch, I hear you're really rich." she began during their next session, "I like that in a man. It shows some brains, and to me it's a big part of a man." That was the best thing Nedra could have said to fat, bald, bug-eyed Butch Russell. Why yes, he was rich. Most people didn't appreciate how smart you had to be to amass such huge quantities of money. "And just how do you get money, Honey?" purred Nedra as she exhaled a big cloud of cigarette smoke. She truly hated being nice to the son-of-a-bitch and she despised calling him "Honey" but, it rhymed.

With that, the floodgates opened, raw sewage poured forth. For years, Butch had wanted to brag to someone about what a great crook he was. He was proud of himself and was busting to brag about his accomplishments. He couldn't tell Joan, his wife. She was thoroughly straight- laced, moral and religious that she would have divorced him and turned him in on the spot.

Here before him was a beautiful naked woman who seemed to really appreciate his talents; a beautiful all but naked girl to whom he proudly disclosed details from decades of corruption and crime. He portrayed himself as the mastermind and the Judge as a willing follower quite naturally.

Nedra played her part, listening in rapt attention oohing and ahhhing at times, remarking that she had no idea he was so smart. It was all an act of course and it became more difficult to keep up the act. Nedra acted through several long sessions but again she had to fight an impulse to throttle the despicable fat rat and choke the very life out of him.

The time came when Nedra had heard more than she wanted to hear so, without explanation to Butch or Dewey she retired as a stripper from **The Fox Pen.** That part of her life was over for good and she was done with it. Years of stripping and saving had built up a fine fund to secure Druisilla's future. The thought of the club disgusted her more than ever. Besides, it was nice to have Friday and Saturday nights to herself.

The next time I walked into the ER, she grabbed my hand and dragged me to the loading dock. "Come on, we need a smoke break." It was the first time Nedra ever touched me! On the loading dock, she began to smoke furiously as she told me that "they" were looting the hospital and, who "they" were. Later she handed me the folder with the same admonishments that I" not tell anyone where I got it from and that I guard it with my life"

I did pore over the documents, but I was not as smart as Nedra nor as well-trained as Sylvia Baker, the accountant. I struggled to understand any subtle financial clues among the pages of mere numbers. The letters and official forms included in the packet were easier for me to grasp. Nedra was recounting the information she tricked out of Butch (although she didn't say where or how she obtained this information of course) and I was starting to understand.

However, life may be altered by unexpected events, this being especially true in life with the volunteer rescue squad.

"I'll tell you what, the Board meets next Thursday night on the first floor boardroom at 7:00 in the evening. Why don't you prepare a short to the point presentation, and I'll see that you get on the agenda." Then Dr. Phillips stood up and shook my hand, thanking me for my service. "By the way, Itsi and Bitsi, my cats are doing well after their surgeries. Thank you for that. Now remember, keep your presentation to ten minutes or less. You lose them after that."

The Hospital Board consisted of eight members, with Butch Russell as the chairman. Al Fusco was there along with two secretaries, one to keep the minutes and the other to do whatever the Board might request. They were all seated around a highly polished oak table. Overlooking one end of the table was a large portrait of General J.E.B. Stuart and at the other end a large painting of R.J. Reynolds, sitting in a chair smoking a cigarette. A remarkable feature in the room was a black waiter in a starched white coat. He stood behind a table on which was a gigantic crystal bowl filled with iced fresh shrimp. There were individual bowls to put the shrimp in and a pile of glistening little shrimp forks, next to which were various seafood sauces. Covering the other half of the table were glasses and whiskey bottles together with many soft drinks and mixers.

After thirty minutes or so the secretary called me into the room. Dr. Phillips smiled cordially as I entered the room. Butch stood up, walked around the table and shook my hand as did Al Fusco. The rest of the Board were lost in their feast of shrimp. Mr. Fusco invited me to join the shrimperee but I declined. I wasn't hungry. I gave my presentation. It took three minutes.

"Those of you who have heard me speak know that I rarely read from prepared notes, but tonight I'm making an exception because I want my remarks to be precise. I will provide copies of my notes to any of you who are interested." I surprised myself at how nervous I was. "On the evening of April 3rd of this year JEB Stuart Volunteer Rescue Squad responded to a single vehicle accident on Paradise Lane in the Bull Mountain Section of the county. There were three victims, two of whom had minor injuries, a thirteen year old female passenger in the vehicle had a severe head injury with a scalp avulsion and a depressed comminuted skull fracture. We thought that we had lost her several times during the difficult extrication from an over-turned vehicle.

"State protocols for Rescue Squads, copies of which I have for your review, dictate that such critically injured patients be transported without delay to a Level One trauma Center. In the case of Patrick County this typically means helicopter transport to North Carolina Baptist Hospital in Winston-Salem.

"On April 3rd and on at least one other occasion, our request for helicopter transport was cancelled by this hospital, presumably by direction of the chief hospital medical officer, Dr. Richter. Dr. Richter may over-rule a state protocol with a local protocol, but such action must be written and properly signed. It must also be submitted to the State Department of Health/ Emergency Services Division in Richmond for review.

"Therefore, as Captain of JEB Stuart Volunteer Rescue Squad I formally request that if this hospital wishes that volunteer rescue squads cease summoning helicopters for the transport of eligible patients, then respectfully, we require a properly written and signed local protocol to that effect.

"I'll be happy to answer any of your questions and I thank you for this opportunity to speak." There were no questions. No one asked for copies of my notes nor for copies of the state protocols.

Butch spoke first. "Are there no questions from the Board?" Well, no. The shrimp-eaters just kept eating their shrimp. "Captain, we greatly appreciate you folks and we appreciate you coming here tonight, and I want to thank you for that, but you need to understand that this hospital may do things in the interest of quality patient care that may seem strange to you. This CAT Scan machine, for example, helps our doctors find out exactly what is wrong with a patient and then they can better decide exactly what to do with that patient. Now that might involve sending them somewhere by helicopter or it might not. The way it works, Captain is that you folks do your thing out there but after you get patients into our facility, we take over and frankly, Captain, what we do with these patients is really not your concern. I hope you understand." Butch was smiling and trying to be as pleasant as possible. He was the one who didn't understand. I wasn't interested in a debate over the virtues of the CAT Scan machine. I was asking for written local protocols and as I began to protest and to repeat my request I was interrupted by Al Fusco, who suddenly stood up flashing his whiter than white smile and firmly shaking my hand. "Thank you again for coming, and we will call you. OK?" Mr. Fusco then quickly and firmly ushered me out of the room. He closed the Board Room door behind me, and I heard a click as he locked it. In that empty hallway I felt very lonely. I had been shined like a highly polished shoe and then thrown out like a dead mouse. I went down to the ER to see Nedra, but she had called in sick. As I walked back to the jeep a feeling of helplessness and powerlessness overcame me. I wasn't handling this well. I was failing my squad and I was failing the patients. It was my responsibility to fix this, but I had no clue how. I was out of ideas. I needed help. As I walked across that empty dark parking lot, even though I didn't know it, help was near.

In the darkest shadow under a tree I heard a proper British accent call out, "You're right, you know." I turned to see the bright red glow of a cigarette and then out of the shadow and into the parking lot lights shuffled a rumpled and disheveled man whom I recognized as one of the shrimp eaters. He wore a nearly white wrinkled suit. The coat could not possibly have been buttoned over the massive expanse of comfortable belly that spilled over his belt and covered his belt buckle. The white shirt had upturned collar points and was adorned by a small black necktie that was tied off-center in a small tight knot. His face was large and pleasant on a huge head with big ears and bushy white eyebrows that constantly jumped up and down over pale blue eyes that danced just like Nedra's. He had a wide mouth and large somewhat yellow teeth. His hair was a riot of white that resembled the curly nest of some rodent. His shoes were dull scuffed loafers that may have been black or brown. He wasn't wearing socks. He was furiously smoking a Camel cigarette holding it between his thumb and two fingers. European style.

"I suggest you find time to visit me at my shop." There was that British accent again. He fished around in his suit coat pocket and handed me a business card with a plump, soft hand.

THE NOOK FOR BOOKS
2314 Main Street, Stuart, Virginia 24171
Andy and Rosalind Pense, Proprietors
We buy and sell books of all types. Come in and read with us.

I put the card in my wallet, thanked Mr.Pense and turned to walk to my jeep. "Cheers!" he called after me. I looked back and saw the furious red glow of the cigarette. As I drove home, I didn't think about the odd encounter in the parking lot. It was the season for odd things and I just figured Mr. Andy Pense was another useless shrimp eater, but then, Andy Pense had made a career of being under- estimated.

CHAPTER EIGHT

Andy and Rosalind

The Judge hated people for the most part, but he was nonetheless interested in them and he enjoyed (if he enjoyed anything) manipulating them to advance his agenda. A hospital board of trustees was useful providing a veneer of legality to the Judge's control of the hospital. His hospital board had to be completely compliant to the Judge's wishes. A truly independent hospital board would review, revise, or reverse any actions taken by the hospital administration. Worse still an out of control board could invite local, state or federal agencies into the hospital to investigate alleged wrong doings. It wasn't enough that, the majority of the board be subservient since a single loud-mouthed member could be troublesome at the least and potentially disastrous to the Judge's agenda.

Brandon Frye was a stocker at the Piggly Wiggly Supermarket. He was selected for the hospital Board because of his lack of education, very limited experience and failure to have ever shown any initiative. He was the perfect candidate for the board based on the Judge's criteria. Brandon was a very earnest young man whose biggest fault was that he never realized that the joke was on him until it was too late. Being appointed to the hospital board was the high point of his entire life. He was invited to join the board in a letter from Butch Russell on hospital stationery complimenting him for his numerous contributions to the community. It was a big deal for Brandon. Then one day a nurse shopping at the Piggly Wiggly approached Brandon.

"Aren't you on the hospital board? Well, I'm a nurse on second floor night shift. Now, don't you dare use my name in this but y'all need to do something about the nurses. They're not being paid enough and y'all don't have enough of 'em on some of the shifts. We had two quit last week and I've heard several of the others say they're thinking about going somewhere else. You can't run the place without nurses. You need to do something. You tell 'em on that board that they better fix this and quick. Now remember" and she grabbed Brandon's arm and squeezed, "you didn't hear none of this from me."

At the next board meeting the members were served roast quail on a bed of seasoned rice. Al and Butch quickly presented some business for a unanimous vote of support. The meeting was almost over when Brandon Frye stood up. It was the bravest thing he had ever done. "Uh, Sirs, uhm," Brandon cleared his throat and coughed into his fist, "excuse me but I have something to say if no one minds, I mean, uh…if I can."

"Who are you?" demanded Butch. Butch had so little contact with the hospital board members on an individual basis that he knew the names of only a few of them. The irritation mixed with contempt in Butch's voice caught Brandon by surprise.

Already nervous, Brandon nearly suffered a complete meltdown. He began to sweat and shake. His voice was oddly high-pitched. "I…I'm …uh… Brandon Frye, sir…and I …uh work I mean I work at the Piggly Wiggly." Brandon felt a bit better so he went on, "Some…uh…a few nurses have told me that…uh…they aren't paid enough and they work too hard and they…uh were wanting…(Oh, God)…for me to…ask…uh…to tell you." Brandon's face was contorted into a hideous grimace. His discomfort was obviously excruciating. "Thank you. Thank you for …uh…well… thank you."

"Thank you, Brandon." It was Al Fusco, speaking quietly and slowly. There was menace in the words. Al leaned forward and showed his whiter than white teeth. It wasn't a smile. It was a predatory rictus such as a badger displays before attacking a small rat. "And thank you for your service to this Board, but your services will no longer be required here. Ever. You can leave now, and I remind you of the confidentiality agreement that you signed. If you discuss hospital business with anyone, the penalties are harsh. You can leave. Now."

Brandon literally fled the room. The other board members scarcely looked up. They were too busy eating their quail and rice. All of his life, Brandon Frye had been warned not to cross certain people in Patrick County and now, he had done just that. He was a nobody. A small fish in a small pond. He drove directly home, locked his doors and windows and went to bed where he hoped and prayed the badgers would forget about him. He hoped he was too small, inoffensive, and unimportant to expect additional punishment. The comfort of his own inadequacy calmed his nerves enough to allow him to fall asleep. The next morning, he was fired by Piggly Wiggly. No reason was given.

The Judge and Butch Russell as owners of the hospital could appoint whomever they chose, and they chose carefully. Extensive background checks were run on each prospective member, but not for the usual reasons. In the case of legitimate boards, the object of appointing members was to recruit talent. On a normal local hospital board expertise in business and finance might be considered a useful background. For example, a Chief Financial Officer of a large company or a banker should make a good board member. An insurance executive with health insurance expertise would be a good addition, as would a retired former government employee after a career handling Medicare and Medicaid claims. Of course, health care professionals should be welcome on any hospital board including retired physicians and nurses or a rescue squad member. A board with such expertise could be expected to effectively and competently manage the affairs of a small local hospital yet these were the very people the Judge did not want on his hospital board. He wanted no one with any background in healthcare whatsoever. In fact, an extensive formal education may be a disqualifying factor. The Judge sought the obedient, the unquestioning, the ignorant and the uncurious; those who saw no reason to doubt or contest what they were told. He wanted underlings instead of bosses; those who had experienced and grown accustomed to the weight of higher authority throughout their lives. While a normal board would seek those with no secret serious sins in their history, such flaws were exactly what the Judge was looking for. Ultimately, the threat of exposing past hidden peccadillos could be a very useful way to exert complete control over any uncooperative board members.

Therefore, the R J R Patrick County Memorial Hospital Board of Trustees was composed of a retired deputy who had been as dishonest as his boss (Sheriff Drew Watson), the owner of a small flower shop who had secretly become pregnant in high school and had given up the child for adoption; a former army sergeant who was hiding a dishonorable discharge due to his alcoholism; a hardware store clerk who sold merchandise off the books; an independent trucker who sold illegal drugs to supplement his income. Now the Judge needed to replace the stocker at the Piggly Wiggly.

"Who are you going to replace that stupid kid with, Butch?" asked the Judge as he and Butch smoked expensive cigars and drank even more expensive whiskey in the Judge's chambers.

"I've been looking at a guy named Andy Pense. He just moved back here from up North. He's retired. He was a professor at some Podunk College in Nowhere, Ohio. He's married to some old English woman. He talks more like a limey than she. They run a bookstore in town. I heard the bookstore's losing money and they're pretty broke. He's real quiet. He's kind of a zero. Not the guy to make waves. Ought to know how to keep his mouth shut. I had him checked out and I think he'll do. We can't keep appointing these dumb kids who don't realize how unimportant they are. I think Mr. Pense realizes exactly how unimportant he is."

On the basis of such a glowing report, Andy Pense was invited to join the hospital board of trustees.

The Judge's system of vetting his board candidates generally worked well but failed miserably in the case of Andy Pense. It wasn't the Judge's fault. Andy's life story was an elaborate lie extensively crafted for his protection and the protection of security interests of the United States of America.

Andrew Ewell Pense was born in 1930 in Patrick County. His father was a logger and a Primitive Baptist preacher. Andy's father gave him a strong sense of morality. Andy was a natural athlete and years of working with his father in the woods gave him strength and coordination. He was an outstanding competitor in high school football, basketball, track, and wrestling. His mother taught school and from her he received a strong sense of humor. She, the teacher, also gifted to her son a deep appreciation for education. Young Andy was blessed with a fine intelligence and his mother began his education early, making sure that he read books on a wide range of subjects. In so doing, she created a lifelong bibliophile.

Andy never looked on his education as a shield against the world (as the Judge did) but as a joyful asset which opened doors to a better understanding of life itself. He won practically every award and honor offered by the Patrick County school system and received a full scholarship to the University of the South in Sewanee. He earned a Phi Beta Kappa key and graduated as the Class Valedictorian. He was awarded a Rhodes scholarship to study for two years at Oxford University. His acceptance was delayed while he served with the Marines in Korea where he acquired a lifelong addiction to cigarettes. At Oxford, he lost his Southern accent and replaced it with a British one. It made him seem more eloquent and educated while a Southern accent typically had the opposite effect. He became quite the Anglophile enjoying rugby, cricket and scotch. For the rest of his life, he would say that he was an Englishman in all but birth.

The casual background check performed by the Judge's associates did indicate that Andy went to college but there was nothing about a Phi Beta Kappa Key, nor was there anything about a Rhodes scholarship, merely that he had "spent some time" in England. There was a military record but no mention of service in Korea nor of awards or decorations. The Judge's background check then revealed that Andy did some post-graduate study at a small private college in Ohio where he settled into a non-stellar career as an Associate Professor of English Literature until his retirement to Patrick County. It was all a lie. A deeper examination dispatching people to perform interviews could have uncovered that Andy Pence was employed around the world by the U. S. Department of State as a "literacy program director" fostering an appreciation for western literature among foreign nationals. That was also a lie.

The elusive truth was that Andy Pence had spent over thirty years as an operative with the CIA. He was one of the best at recruiting and managing human assets (spies) the Agency had at that time. He was a student of human nature and had learned his lessons well. He also had a remarkable ability to quickly master foreign languages. His keen ear for accents enabled him to imitate native speakers. Andy had been directly involved in several of the most important and most successful operations in the agency's history. He was careful to cloak himself in a persona of bookish detachment from world affairs. He never gave the impression of being an accomplished spy master which he was. In the South of the U.S.A., one well-known technique for surviving in difficult situations is to fool your opponents into underestimating you. As I said, Andy made a career of it. He was a man of the shadows and his contributions to this country would be forever hidden, known only to a few but among those few, the accomplishments of Andy Pence would be legendary.

One of his admirers was the future President, George H. W. Bush who had served a short and undistinguished tenure as CIA Director. Andy was assigned to act as a tutor to the politically appointed director. The affable Andy with his British accent and the patrician Bush quickly became more than co-workers; they became close friends. These were bad times for the CIA. American revulsion to excesses of the Vietnam era had crippled United States espionage efforts yet on the other hand, a hard line group of outsiders (appointed by Bush and known as "Team B") was pushing Bush to unleash the full resources of the Agency in an effort to destroy the Soviet Union. Andy was able to provide first-hand examples to Bush of the numerous unheralded successes of covert operations, making a strong case for maintaining such activities even in the face of strong opposition from Congress and, the majority of Americans. Andy had also come to the obvious conclusion that the United States would never triumph over the Soviets in any conventional way, and a military victory would not be worthwhile considering the extreme cost. "We must find a path to rapprochement." advised Andy. "We should bend our efforts not to antagonize them nor undermine them rather with an eye to establishing friendly lines of communication and developing trusted friends among the Soviet elite." It was good advice and "rapprochement" was a word the future President would make his own. Andy held Bush in such high regard that he was the only Republican Andy ever voted for.

As important as his occupation was, the central focus of his life was his wife, Rosalind. Rosalind Taylor-Lee was a native-born Englishwoman who was raised in London as the child of a well-to-do family. From an early age, she wanted to be an actress. She studied drama in London. She had some success, but she never got the break she needed: a big role in a big film. She either had big roles in small movies or small roles in big movies. She had two failed short marriages; one to a gay director and the other to a hopeless drug-addicted actor. Then she found herself in the Philippines working on a best-forgotten Indian spy movie which was a ridiculous knockoff of the Bond films (the lead character was called "Jack Brand, Agent 7-7-0" and her character was "Pussy Cat.") A string band from Bombay performed the score. There was only money for one take so if someone forgot their lines or otherwise messed up, well, it was in the movie. The thing was so god-awful that it was never shown outside the third world.

One beautiful tropical night near Manila, she attended an expatriate party with friends at a diplomat's villa. Rosalind didn't want to go. She had a headache and was exhausted, but her friends were insistent. She stopped by the bar for a scotch on the rocks and retreated to a quiet spot on the veranda, soaking in the warm tropical air and listening to the night sounds from the jungle. The party drifted blissfully into the background.

Suddenly she found herself engaged in conversation with a witty handsome Englishman. She can't remember where he came from. One minute she was sipping her drink by herself on the veranda and the next minute she was laughing at his commentary of life on the Islands. He wasn't an Englishman, it was Andy Pence from Patrick County, Virginia. The mutual attraction was instantaneous; the following year 1965 they were married in Australia. She was twenty-seven, he was thirty-five.

There are no words to describe their relationship. They lived one life in two bodies. It is perhaps enough to say that Rosalind was the only person on earth to truly understand Andy Pence; to know all of his secrets and all of his deepest thoughts. For years they traveled the globe from posting to posting working together. Rosalind took an active role in Andy's work. Often it was her substantial power of persuasion that would bring in an uncertain recruit. She was, after all a practiced actress complimenting espionage with the same deception and suspension of belief found in a great performance. One night in Argentina when it was discovered that an asset had been turned by the opposition and was threatening to give up the entire game to the other side, Rosalind and Andy lured him onto a lonely road, dispatched him with a single pistol shot then disposed of the corpse. Rosalind fired the gun. They each had secrets to keep.

Both loved books and reading. Long evenings were spent reading together smoking and sipping drinks. It was enough to be close to each other. Conversation was unnecessary.

Rosalind had always been one of the most beautiful women in the world with honey hair and sparkling blue eyes, eyes that reflected the light like diamonds. She was small framed which gave a sense of toughness and at the same time vulnerability. As she grew older, she became only more beautiful while stress, good food, cigarettes and time made Andy "comfortably rumpled" as Rosalind described him. If the subject of physical attraction ever came up, Rosalind would smile and pass her open palm over her face, "It's not what's here, Love." she would say and then tapping her temple with her index finger, "It's here." She was beautiful, smart, brave and wise. Taken altogether she was an irresistibly sexy woman. Her heart

They were amused when the victim of an assassination they had engineered would be publicly mourned with a visit to the funeral by the Vice President of the United States. They were bitter when the new regime they installed was as bad or worse than the previous one. They were angry when the demands of the cold war divided the entire planet into "our guys" and "their guys" and "our guys" turned out to be at least as bad as "their guys."

Overall, Rosalind and Andy were proud of their accomplishments. They had the easy confidence of seasoned professionals that could run a covert operation successfully anywhere in any situation. They were eternal optimists in the cosmic struggle of good versus evil, trusting that "good will triumph!" (even though that optimism was tempered by cynicism.)

So what was happening with Patrick County? It was a constant topic of conversation whenever the two were alone. One evening as they prepared for bed they reminisced of past times and adventures. Remembering the African Colonel who two days before a meticulously planned coup became so anxious that he had chest pains and sweats. The poor man seemed to be having a heart attack, but it was a bad case of nerves. For an instant, as Andy watched his future head of state dissolve into a quivering lump of jelly, he thought he should slap the hapless man on his face shake him by the shoulders and say something original like "Get a hold of yourself, Man!" but the thought almost made him laugh and laughing at the poor guy would have made things worse, much worse. So, Andy got right down in the Colonel's face, nose to nose. "Wofa," said Andy in an African dialect, "sometimes when I'm in a tough situation I say to myself 'Buck up-don't fuck up'. Now, you try it".

"What do you say?" asked the Colonel (whose spirits were lifted by any distraction from the task at hand.)

"Buck up. Don't fuck up. Say it over and over again. I've found that it gives courage and resolve. In my country we consider it to be powerful magic. You know, Ju-Ju paa."

"Ju-Ju? Are you serious?" and now both men broke into long laughter. "Andy, you must take me for an idiot but if it works for you…I'll try it, OK?"

"Right" continued Andy, "and if you keep repeating it this coup will be 'cold chop!" (Slang for an easily prepared meal.) The two men embraced, and the coup was a resounding success. Andy was amused at the thought of the Colonel, pistol in hand, leading his troops around the capital chanting "Buck up-don't fuck up. Buck up. Don't fuck up." It was, after all a phrase Andy had made up on the spur of the moment. What fun to recall this adventure!

Then there was the time a Pakistani assassin was scheduled to kill an especially sadistic head of a secret police unit who experienced a similar crisis of nerves. He was vomiting uncontrollably. Rosalind and Andy tried everything to no avail. Their plans seemed in jeopardy. Maybe they would have to seek a replacement trigger man. Then Rosalind put her arm around the heaving body and whispered something in his ear. It was as if a switch was flipped. The poor devil pulled himself together. He hugged Rosalind and kissed her on the cheek. After they dropped their assassin off with his loaded pistol and a hand grenade, Andy asked Rosalind what she had whispered in the man's ear. "I promised to make passionate love to him after this is over." said Rosalind as she exhaled a thick cloud of cigarette smoke. When she noticed the shocked expression on Andy's face she added "Oh don't worry, Love. Remember, we're leaving tonight and besides, he's such an incompetent he'll just get himself killed. Trust me."

She was right on both counts. The operation was a success. This evil head of the secret police was blown to bits removing him as a future threat to Western interests. I suppose success sometimes requires a qualifier. Their work had been morally ambiguous at times. In fact, most of the time.

But what about Patrick County? Where was the anxious Colonel? Where was the nauseated assassin? Yes, they were terrified and intimidated, they were also brave and patriotic. They overcame their fears at great risk and sacrifice to do the right thing, that made them great men, that made them heroes not just to their government but to all humanity in the never-ending struggle of good versus evil. Where were such heroes in Patrick County?

As they tucked into bed, Rosalind said, "I've been giving this a great deal of thought; I've come to the conclusion, it's because the people in Patrick County have too much to lose. Don't you see Andy dear, our former assets overseas lived in intolerable conditions? Their lives must have been absolutely horrid. They had no contact with trusted friends or relatives.

They were isolated and reckoned that death would be preferable to their lives as they were. In short Andy they had nothing to lose."

Andy started to say something, but Rosalind was making her point, "Meanwhile in this place they very much have something to lose, look where they live! This is the most beautiful place in the world. They have to work hard, they're not rich but does it really matter? Most importantly, they're surrounded by friends and family that go back for generations. They're yeomen not peasants: yeomen with some degree of status tied to the land and obliged to support their liege lords. Don't you see? We're in the middle of a feudal system, and our twentieth century methods aren't working."

Once again, Rosalind had asserted her intelligence and her superior insight. She was right of course but Ol' Andy had learned over twenty years ago that right or wrong it did no good to argue a point with her.

They entwined their bodies as they did every night and soon fell fast asleep.

The Judge wasn't sleeping on that rainy night. Instead, he slowly smoked a *La Pearla* cigar and stared out the window of his library into the drizzly darkness. He saw nothing, but he wasn't looking out the window to see anything, he was just staring, trying to think. He was wearing green silk pajamas, leather slippers and a blue smoking jacket, his usual nighttime attire unless he was entertaining visitors, in which case he wore one of his many impeccable black suits, white shirt and red tie. It was his constant uniform. The Judge was never seen in casual attire and he didn't even own a pair of blue jeans. His wardrobe distinguished him from the rest of the community.

Most of us lived in jeans and slept buck naked or in our drawers.

"John!" called out the Judge, "Bring me a Kahlua. Make it a double."

John Powers appeared at the library door. "Right away, Judge. Can I get you anything else, Sir?" In all his years of service, John Powers worked until the Judge told him he could go. There were no regular hours. John hated the job and he hated the man, but he knew that if he complained he would be fired and if he was fired or quit, there's no telling what that crazy old man might do. John Powers knew better than anyone that the only way to get along with the Judge was to do everything he wanted exactly as he wanted it done, and if you didn't get along with the Judge, then he was capable of extreme retaliation. Over decades of listening from his post in the dining room John Powers had heard the Judge direct false arrests, economic destruction and even the murder of those he found objectionable. Those who stood in his way.

On this night, the Judge was seething with murderous anger due to his potentially lethal betrayal by two of his closest associates.

Butch Russell and Al Fusco were in the Judge's way as no one had ever been. "Just bring me the drink and then you can go home." In all the long years of service, the Judge had never offered a pleasantry to John Powers. Never a thank you, a how are you, a please, a hello or even a simple good night. Their relationship was strictly that of master-servant. At times John Powers wondered if the use of his name was a coincidence as it was traditional in the South for white men to address black men as "John."

So, John Powers left the Judge alone with his drink and his cigar, gazing at nothing. There was no point in listening from the dining room. Except for the ticking of the old clock, the room was silent.

Inside the Judge's head things were loud. The Judge imagined inviting Butch and Al to his library the very room in which he now stood. He would offer them expensive cigars and whiskey. No, more than that, he would invite them to a great meal, a veritable feast. After the meal he would lead them into the walnut paneled library for cigars and whiskey. Yes. That's how he would do it. Here my boys, let's enjoy the benefits of our labors. The privileges of wealth. Immense wealth. Then the Judge would talk to them pleasantly, complimenting them on their performance and remarking how clever they are. Oh, how clever you are, my boys. So clever as to figure out how to loot my goddam hospital right under my very nose!

The Judge imagined their frozen smiles, their looks of panic then the Judge would pull out a pistol, a big pistol and he would leap up from his chair and shoot Al Fusco at point blank range right between the eyes blowing his brains out from the back of his head in an explosion of crimson. The gunshot in such a room would be deafening.

With his ears ringing the Judge would turn to Butch. He envisioned Butch paralyzed with terror at the violent death inflicted on his partner in crime. He would start to cry and blubber as he stared at the near-headless corpse still seated in the fine leather chair. Gun smoke would linger in the room as the Judge accosted Butch. "You silly, little son of a bitch. Didn't

I do enough for you? Didn't I make you everything that you are or ever will be? And yet you would steal from me? From me? Beg, filthy bastard! Get down on your damn knees and beg me for your life! Plead with me to spare you from Hell!" The Judge would say. And the Judge knew Butch would beg. The fat little bug-eyed pervert would sob and beg. He would vomit up his fancy dinner. He would urinate into his own suit. The Judge would demand that he lick his boots and his foot and then command him to stop because he's not fit to lick his feet, even the boot without a foot in it belonging to the Judge, his master, his liege lord. It would be in that moment of extreme humiliation, in that state of ultimate degradation that the Judge would slowly cock the big black pistol and shoot Butch Russell in the top of his head. The Judge would put the muzzle in contact with the skin so that the scalp itself would burn around the hole into the skull. Yes. That's how he would do it. That would be his retribution. Their atonement for such greed and stupidity. Yes, that's what would happen. The Judge smiled his quick tight grimace. As he smiled, he knew that it would never happen. The Judge had to be smarter. He had to be more subtle, but still, it was a pleasant thought.

Two weeks later, Andy came home from a hospital board meeting. "I may have found someone who can help us." he said to Rosalind as he kissed and hugged her.

Rosalind looked at her husband with sparkling blue eyes. "Oh, and whom might that be?"

"He's a bit idealistic and naïve. I don't think he's an intellectual giant by any means but he's well-placed. He's the captain of the JEB Stuart Rescue crew. He's not one of your hereditary yeomen. I don't know how we overlooked him."

"Well, good for you and good for us; but it is a bit late and I'm exhausted for some reason. I think we should go to bed and try again in the morning" said Rosalind as she started upstairs to the bedroom. In minutes they were asleep. Sleep however, didn't last through the night and they were awakened by a bright red flashing light filling their room. One habit they had was to sleep in the" buff" so the naked couple crept out of bed and peered cautiously from their bedroom window. They were looking down on the JEB Stuart ambulance as it backed up to the entrance of the apartment next door.

"Oh dear," remarked Rosalind, "I hope nothing has happened to Mrs. Perry." Sally Perry was a seventy-year old retired fourth grade teacher. She and Bertha Jones had taught in the same school for nearly thirty-five years. The two naturally gravitated toward each other. Both were natives of Patrick County and both had married their work instead of a man. They stood together on the playground, they ate together in the cafeteria and most nights they were together, eating at different restaurants, going to movies or visiting each other for home cooked meals and television; and yes, something had in fact happened to Miss Sally Perry. She had suffered from a deep pain in her left arm for about a week. Sally assumed she had injured the arm somehow but tonight she had awakened with severe shortness of breath and sweating. There was no chest pain, but these were the classic symptoms of a heart attack in a woman.

The call came in at 2:15 a.m. When Bertha Jones heard the address, she signed on immediately. I was up anyway, so I signed on and then Earl Ashe signed on to make a full crew. Earl was a greasy-haired, pale skinned kid whom I figured was a vampire of some kind. That would explain why he was awake at such an early morning hour.

When we arrived at the scene, Earl backed the ambulance up to the door while I followed Bertha inside. Miss Perry was seated in a large old armchair in her modest living room. She wore a nightgown under a flannel robe. She had sensible slippers made from leather that were likely intended for a man. Her eyes were wide and panicky. Her skin was glistening with a drenching sweat that was raining off her body. She was taking rapid deep breaths with an audible gasp. Her color was the gray patina of death.

"Sally! What on earth is wrong with you?" Shouted Bertha as she entered the apartment. (Sally required shouting at because she was nearly deaf.) "Doc, you and Earl get the cot and the oxygen while I check out this old faker."

"I don't know what all's wrong with me, Bertha. I just can't catch my breath and my heart seems to be running away in my chest." Then Sally Perry looked at her old friend square in the eyes. "Am I going to die, Bertha? Tell me the truth."

Bertha had been applying a blood pressure cuff to Sally's arm, but she stopped and stared right back at Sally. "Yes, Sally! You are going to die!"

"Yes, we know something about RJR, Inc. actually we need documents. As you say, 'we need it in writing'."

"But I have documents. Copies of contracts, agreements and cancelled checks."

"What? What did you just say? You have documents? In your possession? You can show them to me, of course. And where did you get them?" Andy's face lit up. He was the philatelist who discovers the upside-down airplane stamp between the pages of an old book. The art collector who finds a long- lost Picasso at a yard sale. The history buff who inherits Jack Ruby's snub-nosed .38. Andy was a man who had spent his entire life finding and using precious bits of information and I was telling him about the existence of a treasure. Ecstasy is a poor word to describe Andy's state of mind.

"They're in a safe place. I got 'em from a nurse at the hospital. To be honest about it, I haven't really had the time to read it all and what I've read I haven't fully understood."

"Listen to me." now it was Rosalind speaking as she grasped both my hands in hers. Her hands were smooth, soft and strong all at the same time. "You must bring everything you have to us tomorrow night, and you must bring your nurse as well. By the way, you're not lovers, are you?"

"No. Just friends"

"Good. Makes things less complicated." Observed Andy. "On that note, I've got to spend a penny." Andy shambled down the hall in a thick cloud of cigarette smoke.

Rosalind collected our empty glasses on the silver tray. "Can I get you another drink or something, Love?"

"No thank you, ma'am. I've got to go, anyway. It's pretty late and I'm out past my bedtime."

"Please wait until we can both tell you goodbye. You've been so kind", and she turned toward the kitchen, leaving me alone and cozy in my little corner of the shop. As I sat, I reached out my arm and took a random book from the nearby shelf. It was titled *Walk Egypt*, a novel written by Vinnie Williams and published by Viking Press in 1960. I opened to the first page and was soon lost in the words:

The woman's name was Toy, and it suited her no more than silk

on Sunday or the cotton she wore the rest of the week. Silk and
cotton are amenable fabrics, easy to the hand and accepting a bit
of lace or ruffle. The woman was like linen, strong and reticent...

I had fallen under the magical spell of the little book shop. The magical spell of the bookshop, its books and its owners.

I went to the hospital as quickly as I could and caught up with Nedra in the parking lot. Fortunately, she had a late case and she was about a half hour late leaving work or I would have missed her. She looked genuinely glad to see me. I had been very busy and our meetings on the loading dock had become few and far between. I missed her.

"How you? Hey...uh...I met this couple that want to meet you tomorrow night at the little bookstore in Stuart. Can you be there about 9 o'clock?"

"What?" Nedra was half-laughing. "No. I can't be anywhere at 9 o'clock tomorrow. I've got to work. What's this all about, anyway?"

"He's a member of the hospital board and he wants to talk to you about the papers you gave me."

"Oh no, no, no!" Nedra was now genuinely mad. "I did my part. I handed that stuff over to you. You're on your own there, Big Boy. I read what's in those papers. It's dynamite and I know how things work around here. Messin' around with those papers could get me fired or worse. See you later. I'm tired and I gotta go home."

"Nedra, please. You told me you cared about these patients and you do. I know you do. Nobody ever has to find out you were involved. I'll come by and pick you up. We can ride together. Please. These are good people. They can help. Please, Nedra..."

"Oh, there's a great idea! You, and me go ridin' around Stuart at night together. I'd not only get fired but everybody would call me a home wrecker and a whore. Sorry, Man, I got a kid to think of and she means more to me than anything."

"It's precisely because you have Drusilla that you ought to come with me. These guys are going to wreck the hospital and if there's no hospital and something happens to Dru, God forbid, you'll have to take her all the way to Martinsville, and you'll have to take her yourself 'cause I won't be able to recruit volunteers and we'll lose these rescue squads if they have to go all the way to..."

"Who are these bookstore people anyway? Has it ever occurred to you that they might be spies working for the other side and they might just be settin' you up? Look, I know how things work around here. You're acting like a real dumbass and you can count me out." She was really mad. The black eyes were dancing a war dance.

"Damn it all! Damn it Nedra! Damn all y'all! Fusco and Russell are bad guys and they're screwing you over and nobody'll stand up to 'em and that's all you gotta do, just stand up to 'em! Here's your chance. Nothing bad's gonna happen but if you lose your job, hell, I'll hire you. Think about it. Sometimes you have to do a tough or scary thing for no better reason than it's the right thing to do. You really need to talk to this couple at the bookstore and yeah, I'm sure they're spies of some kind, but I don't think they're working for Mr. Fusco or..." I couldn't believe I was talking to her like this.

"Shhhh! Not so loud!" She was noticeably calmer, she smiled. "So, what are you saying? You'd make me a doggie nurse? Seriously? I make more money than you do. I don't think you can pay me enough to put up with you. Besides, you're kind of an asshole."

"I'm really sorry. I shouldn't have said all..."

"I'll be there, all right? I'll call in sick and I'll drive myself. Bookstore in Stuart, nine o'clock. Right?"

"Thanks, I..."

"Just shut up. You won the argument. Now just shut up. But listen, if one person, I mean anybody at all finds out about this, I'll kill your ass. You hear me? I'll cut off your balls. Looks like they're too big for you to handle anyway." She winked at me as she closed her car door.

I watched the red taillights disappear into the night and I never wanted anyone so much in my life.

The next night she was late, and for a while I was afraid she had changed her mind, but then she knocked on the door. Rosalind and Andy greeted her. Andy embraced her in a bear-hug, and she rolled her dancing eyes. What had I gotten her into?

As we settled into our over-stuffed chairs, Rosalind served Andy and me some sort of strong, sweet, dark liqueur and she and Nedra had tall glasses of iced tea. Rosalind had first thought of iced tea as an abomination but with Andy's tutelage she became used to it.

We talked about ourselves and the unseasonably warm weather until Rosalind picked up the thick folder of documents. "How did you come by this, Darling?"

"I can't say." replied Nedra.

"But surely you can confide in us. We may wish to talk to that person ourselves." Tension was introduced into our little group as Nedra bristled at Rosalind's persistence. I had first-hand experience with Nedra's temper. Our little committee could blow apart before it got started.

"Look, I didn't want to come here from the get-go and…" she moved forward in her chair as if she were about to stand up. Stand up and walk out.

"You're absolutely right, my Dear." interrupted Andy as he reached over and lightly touched Nedra's wrist. "You should keep your promises. You shouldn't betray your source; and now we know that you won't tell anyone about us. I assure you we shall never tell anyone about you."

With Nedra settled back in her chair, Rosalind opened the folder and began to verbally review the documents page by page being certain that we all understood the information and that we all came to the same conclusions. It became an animated three-way discussion. I was the kid who hadn't done his homework, so I had little to contribute to the conversation. I also realized that in this battle of wits, I was woefully under-gunned. I expected as much from Rosalind and Andy but, I was surprised at Nedra's knowledge of accounting practices and contract law. Then I remembered that at one time she had worked for a bank in Winston. Or so she said.

On several occasions, Andy or Rosalind would ask, "What were they thinking?" and then to our amazement, Nedra would tell us exactly what they were thinking.

"How do you know that?" asked Andy at one point.

Of course, Nedra didn't mention **The Fox Pen** or how much information a naked beautiful woman can extract from a dirty old pervert. "Butch is my ex-father-in-law and he likes to run his mouth and he brags a lot. And he's stupid!"

"I have to agree with you on that last observation." chuckled Andy.

It was one-thirty in the morning before we were finished. The session had been interrupted only by trips down the hall to the "loo" and Rosalind refreshing our drinks and offering us biscuits (cookies) and crackers with cheese. We agreed to meet again on Friday night.

"Are you sure this is no imposition?" Andy asked Nedra.

"No. This is important."

By the time we hugged our goodbyes at the door of the little shop we were four co-conspirators. Co-conspirators and friends.

"Good night, Doc." said Nedra as we parted. I watched her walk down the dark street and get into the sleek black BMW. At that moment, I would have done anything in the world for that woman. I also wondered how she could afford such a car. Maybe nurses did make more money than veterinarians.

As I drove through the night to my house, I was aware that I was intoxicated, by the strong liqueur. I smiled to myself. Now I was a drunk driver.

Once I got home, I crept quietly into the house and slipped into bed.

"Who have you been out fucking?" asked Glenda. "Carolyn Miller or that nigger nurse at the hospital?"

"Don't use that word."

"If she's just a nurse at the hospital, she's an African-American but if she's fucking my husband, she's a nigger."

I'm certain that Glenda's rant continued along the lines of what an awful husband I was and what a low-life son of a bitch she was married to, but I passed out into a dreamless sleep.

On Friday, I was a little late getting to the book shop. A dog had been hit by a car and then there had been a rescue squad call. Andy met me at the door. Rosalind and Nedra were engaged in an animated discussion about ornamental flowers.

Once we settled down to business, Andy led us through a complete review of the documents. He was aggressively chain smoking, keeping a bright red coal on the end of each cigarette and a cloud of gray smoke around us. "Now. What we must do is to separate what we know, that is what we can document in writing, from what we think, our speculations, conclusions and hear-say. Are you with me? Good. Next we have to carefully plan what action, if any, we should take keeping in mind that we're out to kill the King and if you're out to kill the King you bloody well need to properly prang the bugger." He crushed out his cigarette and immediately lit another with a shiny Zippo lighter adorned with the Marine Corps insignia. *Semper Fi*. So old Andy had been a Marine. He would never cease to surprise me.

We all agreed that whatever the risk, we wanted to "Kill the King." We could document that Butch and Al were looting the hospital to the point of endangering the place financially. We knew that this was done by the creation of RJR, Inc. a dummy corporation with the sole purpose of skimming profits from the hospital by adding fees to employees' salaries, renting equipment to the hospital that the hospital once owned, and charging exorbitant fees for a CAT scan machine that the hospital had been improperly tricked into buying and then turning over to RJR Inc. We had the documents. We knew these things. We also knew that RJR. Inc. paid Butch and Al around $600,000.00 each year in addition to whatever other income they may have enjoyed.

We "supposed" that this activity was embezzlement. We also "supposed" that helicopter calls were being cancelled in order to funnel insured accident victims into the CAT scan machine. Furthermore, we "supposed" that The Judge was unaware of what Butch and Al were up to and we "supposed" that The Judge, who liked complete control over his County, would not be happy.

"You see" said Rosalind, "this Judge, while truly despicable in his own right, could be an ally of convenience for us. After all, we want the same thing: Butch and Al punished and RJR, Inc. out of the hospital."

"Exactly" continued Andy. "Remember, we don't know to whom we should report our suspicions. We don't know how far the Judge's tentacles extend, and until we decide an overall plan of action, we should be careful not to tip our hand. We're setting a trap and we don't want to set the trap off prematurely and give away the game."

Nedra asked "Why don't y'all just tip off the Judge and let 'em tear each other apart."

"That was my next point." replied Andy. "Are we all in agreement that I should forward some of these documents to the Judge?"

"I can't believe the Judge doesn't know something about what's going on, but from what I've heard about the guy, if he knew everything that's in these documents, Butch and Fusco would already be dead." observed Nedra.

"Of course, we don't know for sure that the Judge isn't actually involved with the whole scheme. He wouldn't be the first thief to steal from himself." added Rosalind.

"No. That's not the case. Butch is scared to death that the Judge is going to find out about this deal. Really!" Nedra did have special insights into Butch Russell's mind.

"So, we all agree to tip off the Judge?" asked Andy again. We all agreed.

"Next, we need to put the hospital at the front of the public consciousness. That's where the helicopters and the rescue squads come in. This subject is already in the public's eye thanks to all the scanners that monitor radio calls. In many homes, listening to the scanners was a popular evening pastime. There's no point in talking to the Patrick County press; but the regional press is a different situation. I think this story has legs and it should grasp the public's attention. Now, once we've got their attention, I'll present the documents to the hospital board as a board member, and to the press. I think the board will be forced to fire Fusco and Butch and demand an investigation. That should be about as much as we can do." Andy had it all planned out.

"Doc," Rosalind was speaking directly to me, "there is a reporter with the Martinsville newspaper. Her name is Brittany Hayes. You should call her tomorrow and set up an appointment for an interview."

"Remember" warned Andy, "stick to just what you know personally and that would be the rescue squad and the canceling of your helicopter calls. Come back before our board. You want a written variance of state regulations or they should stop interfering with you. It makes them appear unreasonable. Don't wade into this RJR thing. It could be more of a quagmire than we now realize so don't mention it."

No one had mentioned money laundering because none of us knew anything about the money laundering. It wasn't in our documents. Andy was right about one thing: it was a quagmire and I was about to dive in headfirst.

The next day Rosalind mailed a large brown envelope marked "Private and Personal" to the Judge. Inside were copies of all the documents we had.

"You know: Why? What's the motivation for the hospital to cancel helicopter calls? Who benefits? It certainly doesn't seem to be in the hospital's interests to endanger the well-being of their patients." She was really enjoying her salad.

I thought about Andy's directions that I stick to helicopters, ambulances and car wrecks. "Well, I don't have any idea as to why." I lied. "Does it matter?"

"The hospital says that they cancel helicopter calls in order to have time enough to use their new machine to better decide whether or not they need to send the patient off to a higher level trauma center and if so where the patients should best be sent. I've got to tell you, as a layman, that argument sounds reasonable to me." She blotted her mouth with the corner of her napkin, I noticed that she wore a bright red shade of lipstick that complimented her white complexion.

"If their case is so strong why not produce a written protocol for it? They've really put the squads in a bind: we either challenge the hospital or we violate state regulations." I was about to explode.

"I see your concern but there's no story here. You say this. They say that and that's that. If I write this story, it'll get stuck in the back pages for filler and nobody will read it. I'm a top-flight journalist and I'd rather spend my time writing stories that our readers care about. This isn't it. Are you sure you don't know of another reason they're blocking helicopter calls? Come on. Take a guess."

I noticed that as beautiful as her eyes were, she never looked directly at me. She was always looking at something else. It was a good interviewing technique because it created a desire in the interviewee to say something outrageous to attract her attention. It worked on me.

"Money."

"Excuse me?"

"Money. They cancel the helicopter calls so they can make money."

"How so?" She stopped eating her salad and placed a small tape recorder on the table between us.

"Mr. Fusco and Mr. Russell set up a company called RJR, Inc. to skim the profits out of the hospital. The company also owns that obsolete CAT scan machine and they make a bunch of money if they scan victims of

Ms. Brittany Hayes, reporter for the Patrick and Pittsylvania Coun at the Martinsville newspaper was by most measures, insane. She been in the grip of obsessive-compulsive disorder for all her 27 years. a child, she didn't play with her toys, she arranged them. In school, was the student who would stay up all night if necessary, completing assignment such as a term paper or special project that might not be du for weeks. At Randolph-Macon, she couldn't find a roommate that suited and she went through a half-dozen before she was finally assigned a singl occupancy room. She was past being a neat freak. Everything had to be just right, not just in proper order but the same proper order it had been in yesterday. She was naturally nosey about other people's business, so she chose to pursue a career in journalism, attending graduate school at Old Dominion University.

She was attractive enough. She had wide baby blue eyes and short blond hair kept in a bob not so much for stylish reasons but because it was easy to look the same perfect way each day. She had several serious boyfriends but after sex she would hop out of bed and take an immediate shower then shoo the poor suitor out of bed and change the sheets. It was hardly surprising that she had never married.

When I arrived at her desk in the newsroom of the paper, she immediately glanced at her watch, announced it was nearly two o'clock and ordered me to accompany her to lunch. She always ate lunch at the same restaurant at the same small table at two o'clock in order to avoid the lunchtime crowds. It wasn't lost on me that her desk was perfectly neat while the other desks in the room were a jumble. I later learned that some of her colleagues enjoyed moving her stapler and her pencil cup to see how many seconds (yes, seconds) would pass after she returned to her desk before correcting the mental chaos. Her clothes were as neat as her desk. She wore a white blouse buttoned to the top and a black business suit daily.

At the restaurant, she ordered the vegetarian salad without dressing and black coffee. I had a glass of Pepsi. "Speak to me." She commanded as she ate her salad. I told her about helicopters, ambulances and car wrecks; how my helicopter calls had been cancelled and how I needed written signed variances to override state protocols.

"Why?"

"Why? I'm not sure I understand..."

automobile accidents. It doesn't do a damn thing for the patient except to delay transport to competent care. They're looting the hospital."

"Atta boy! Now you're getting it!" She smiled for the first time and now she looked directly at me. Her smile was beautiful, and I was attracted to her by it. If she had offered to finish the interview at her place I would have, and she could take all the showers and change all the sheets she wanted to. "Tell me more."

And stupidly I did. I told her everything I knew. I ignored everything Andy had warned me against. I got carried away and acted like a total idiot. I didn't so much dive headfirst into the quagmire as I belly-flopped. What a fool I was.

By four o'clock, lunch and the interview were over and she had her story. On the front page of the Sunday edition was a large headline:

Rescue Squad Chief:
'They're Looting Our Hospital!'

Below the headline was the whole story exactly as I told it. I wasn't misquoted. It was all my fault. I went to the book shop to apologize to Andy and Rosalind. I knew they were angry, but Andy just said, "What's done is done. We'll have to make the best of it."

Andy requested a special meeting of the hospital board of trustees, presented the documents to the group and made a motion that the Board immediately terminate Mr. Fusco's contract and ask for a criminal investigation by an outside prosecutor. He also expressed the opinion that Mr. Russell should resign from the board. There was no second on his motions. Butch Russell stared coldly at Andy and said only that he would entertain a motion for adjournment. A few days later, Andy received a letter informing him that his service on the hospital board was no longer required.

The article written by Brittany Hayes was picked up and reprinted in every major newspaper in the region. People were concerned about the sky-rocketing costs of health care and their inability to pay, even when insured. There seemed to be no identifiable cause for it. It certainly didn't seem to be greed on the part of doctors and nurses; but here was this report of a hospital administrator in a small rural hospital who may have been making as much as a million dollars a year! What if all the hospital administrators were doing the same thing? Well, heck, that's what's wrong with the system! They're lootin' the hospitals! All the hospitals! Suddenly there was a simple solution to a complex problem and people love that. They love reading about it and to read about it, they had to buy newspapers. The story, as they say, took on a life of its own. Editorials and commentators on television and radio fanned the flames.

My parking lot became full as did my veterinary hospital, not so much with clients and their pets as with people wanting to shake my hand and slap me on the back. "Way to go! God Bless you!" It was the same thing anywhere I went in public. I was mobbed by well-wishers.

I gave telephone interviews to newspapers in Roanoke, Richmond, New Port News, Winston-Salem, Greensboro, Raleigh and even the *Washington Post*. In addition, I appeared on numerous television and radio programs around the region. Strangers were recognizing me on the street. I had become a celebrity. A miniscule celebrity but a celebrity none the less and as I became more practiced at it, I warmed to my subject. In interviews I referred to Butch and Al as not just "looters" but as "liars, crooks and thieves." I ranted indignantly about their profiteering on the backs of the sick and injured. I all but accused them of robbing widows and orphans at gun point.

Maybe Andy was wrong. Maybe we should have gone public right from the start. Nothing like sunlight to put the rats on the run, eh? Surely, surely the rich and powerfully elite in Stuart couldn't withstand the waves of adverse publicity crashing over them. It was simple. You just have to stand up to them.

There is no reliable account of the Judge having any contact with Butch or Al during this time. The old heron just stood poised in the shallow water at his end of the pond. Waiting, watching, planning, thinking; yet all the while seemingly detached from events and no more concerned or involved than the surrounding reeds.

Butch Russell was frantically trying to salvage the situation. He had control over the Patrick County radio station and the newspaper, but in bordering counties, freedom of the Press was more robust. Editors and commentators knew a hot topic when they saw one. Patrick Countians were more than eager to call or write in with their personal stories of excellent care at the RJR Hospital and timely transport by the rescue squads and helicopters to salvation at large medical centers. There were others who had been financially destroyed by hospital bills they could never hope to pay and when they found out that their tormentors were Butch and Al and that the money wasn't designated for medical care at all but for lavish undeserved lifestyles a white hot anger was ignited within them.

A rich vein of hidden pent-up resentment had been tapped. The Russell's, the Watsons and the Judge's family had been lording it over the county as robber barons for generations. That's why granddaddy's liquor still was destroyed. That explains why Uncle Jack lost his farm due to some technicality at a Russell-owned bank and was sold for next to nothing to a Watson. It all made sense. As the stories were exchanged among friends, neighbors and relatives it became clear that they had been living under the boot heel of oppression. The whole county.

The three families were not only blamed for actual sins committed but for every incidence of bad luck, tragedy, or hard time in the recent history of Patrick County. "We have been nothing but a bunch of sheep and by God, we ain't sheep." Put another way, that old dog who had been kicked and beaten for so many years was about to bite. The white, hot anger had reached a heat that would melt chains.

Butch decided that a public meeting should be held at the high school. They could talk to people and the people would nod their heads in agreement and return to their normal lives. He would call it a "Community Meeting" and it was advertised with posters and on the local radio and in the local newspaper. It had always worked in the past but this time it was a bad idea. If the entire population of the County is turning into a lynch mob, the last thing you want to do is tell 'em exactly when and where they can find you.

The high school auditorium was packed. On the stage was a long table and three chairs each with a microphone. There were no microphones available to the audience. Whatever the audience might say was not to be heard. The show began twenty minutes late, giving the anger in the crowd time to simmer as rumors were exchanged with the citizen in the next seat. Then out onto the stage filed three men in business suits. There was Butch Russell, Ralph Jones the chairman of the Patrick County Board of Supervisors and Al Fusco. The Honorable Mr. Jones spoke first.

"I want to thank, each and every one of you for coming tonight. It's been an unusual week here in Patrick County and I think that there is a lot of misinformation circulating out there; we thought we'd just get everybody together and tell you the truth. As we all know truth is hard to find in the liberal media outside Patrick County." Ralph made a small, nervous laugh. No one laughed with him. Butch and Al sat stone-faced. "Now with me tonight are two of the finest men in this County. Men who have worked tirelessly to provide health care here and their efforts have not been in vain. We are very lucky to find such wonderful gentlemen who have selflessly given of themselves for you." With that a ripple of derisive laughter passed through the crowd. "There are always a few trouble-makers out there who try to bring down such gentlemen and hurt their work, but the Bible says we must allow free speech to everyone, so we do that, but lies are lies. You all know these two prominent members of our community. I'll introduce them to you anyway and then they'll explain everything. They'll address your concerns about the hospital and drive off these liars and fear mongers just like Moses ran the money lenders off the temple steps.

"To my right is The Honorable Mr. William Russell Esquire, our Commonwealth's Attorney and the Chairman of the Hospital Board of Trustees." There were boos in the crowd. People were booing a Russell! "To my left is our hospital administrator, The Honorable Mr. Albert Fusco. Let's welcome them and show them your appreciation with your applause." With that, Ralph stood up and was beaming a broad smile as he turned to first one and then to the other esteemed guest. The two Honorable dignitaries looked stone-faced and waved weakly as if they were royalty receiving the adulation of their subjects. Trouble is, the subjects weren't adulating. There was some polite applause but there were more boos and hisses and a few shouted remarks which were difficult to hear over the noise.

Butch cleared his throat and pulled his microphone closer leaning into it which produced a sharp squeal of feedback. "Thank you, Mr. Jones. Thanks to all of you for coming out tonight. What you people need to understand is that those of us in these positions know better than anyone about how to conduct the business of the hospital and when we make decisions about how to conduct that business then we should not be questioned about it. It's counter-productive and it makes Patrick look bad to our neighbors. I don't tell you how to run your business and you shouldn't be telling me how to..."

"It's not your business! That hospital is our business!" Came a shout from the back of the crowded auditorium.

"You ain't runnin' it! You're lootin' it!" cried another.

From all over the room came shouts of "Yeah!" and "Right on!"

One older woman struggled to her feet and in a high, reedy voice said, "We all paid for that hospital and I don't know who turned it over to you and that damn yankee..."

"Wait just a minute!" Butch was red-faced and his bulging eyes looked about to pop out of his head. "We haven't looted anything. You can't have profits in a non-profit hospital! We had to get rid of the excess profit, but it's safe! The money's safe!"

"Yeah! Safe in your pockets!" Now the crowd was mostly on their feet and many were shouting at the three men on stage.

A tall man in front called out in a voice that rose above the din "You're nothin' but thieves! All of ya' are nothin' but thieves! Ya' oughta be in jail!"

"You shut up!" commanded a blood red and sweating Butch. In retrospect, it was a particularly stupid thing to say to an angry crowd.

Enough can be enough and with a single roar, the mob rushed the stage. "Get 'em!" and "Let's shake our money out of 'em!" Some shouted out "Kill 'em!"

There were only two deputies in attendance. Butch had requested six or more plus a State Trooper but the Judge had quietly countermanded that order and told the Sheriff to only send two. "The smallest two you have." The Judge knew Patrick County and he knew what might happen at Butch's so-called "Community Meeting."

The three men in business suits made an unseemly retreat through the back door of the stage and were bundled into the back seat of a patrol car by the two frightened deputies. The mob was right on their heels as the car sped off with lights and siren.

All the lights and windows were broken out of Al Fusco's car, and Butch Russell's shiny black Cadillac was over-turned and set on fire. Ralph Jones drove an old high-mileage Chevy, and no one could be sure which one was his so Ralph's car was left undamaged.

The anger of the County burned white hot and searing. It seared the very foundations of control built up so patiently over so many decades.

The next day, Sheriff Frank Watson appeared on all the regional television news casts blaming the riot on "outside agitators." I don't know. I wasn't there.

Solomon Brandon Fields was born and raised in Cleveland, Ohio. He never knew who or where his father was. His mother was a kindergarten teacher who was enthusiastic and happy to the point of annoying. After fifteen minutes with that woman most people wanted to shake her and tell her to "Please shut up!" Brandon, as he was called, grew up in a house with two maiden aunts, his mother and the matriarchal widow of Solomon Fields, his grandmother. You might say the boy never had a chance.

Brandon was desperate for attention as a boy and was fascinated by radio and television personalities. They seemed to get attention. After high school, Brandon set out to pursue his dream, but he had a slight speech impediment (a lisp) and he tried too hard. Instead of working his way up the career ladder, he started near the bottom and worked his way down. He hit rock bottom as station director and DJ (he preferred the term "radio personality") at WJJP in Stuart, a small facility owned and controlled by the Judge.

He had a local morning talk show called "Fields Good in the Morning!" every weekday during which he would discuss subjects of interest with different guests. One day it might be the extension agent advising you on how to safely can meats. Another day, a pest control expert would talk about controlling the scourge of Japanese Beetles. Sometimes, it would be the Madam President of the Shady Grove Women's Club discussing the Club's latest project and seeking new members. I was surprised when Brandon called and asked me to be one of his guests. Stupidly, I agreed.

I had heard that the Judge owned the radio station, but I didn't comprehend just what that meant. I figured that my story was newsworthy and that WJJP, especially after the riot at the high school auditorium, was anxious to put me on the air. After all, I had given many interviews and they had all gone well and had furthered my cause.

Brandon Fields had a constant smile filled with glistening white even teeth. His hair was slicked straight back and held in place by some shiny hair oil. He wore a cheap suit, or at least it looked cheap. His eyes betrayed him. They were the brown terrified eyes of a trapped rabbit. Brandon Fields was scared. I didn't know why he was scared, but he was scared.

We sat at a small table as the show started. Brandon was the only full-time employee. He had several tape decks sitting around all cued up for advertising and other useful announcements. He started one of these cassettes. The room and the airwaves filled with loud toneless banjo music which was evidently Brandon's theme song.

"Gooood Morning Patrick County! It's time for Fields Good in The Morning! I'm your host Brandon Fields and with me today is the Captain of the JEB Stuart Volunteer Rescue Squad! But first a word from one of our sponsors!" During the commercial for an appliance store owned by the Russell's, Brandon sat with a fixed smile on his face and when I started to say something, he put his finger to his lips. Evidently you could hear what we said even during commercials.

Once the show started, Brandon didn't waste any time. Everything he said was in a shout. I never listened to his show. I thought he was annoying but, he was about to become much more annoying.

"And with me this beautiful Patrick County morning is our local veterinarian, and, the Captain of the JEB Stuart Volunteer Rescue Squad! Welcome, Sir!"

"Thank you and it's a pleasure to…" I started but didn't get to finish.

"Many people around here think that all this trouble we've been having, the discord at our hospital, riots at the high school and so forth is your fault! That you're responsible! What do you think?"

"Well I hope it's not my fault I was just trying to…"

"Now let me get this straight! You think the hospital administration is cancelling helicopters so that they can use the new CAT scan machine! Is that right?" Brandon retained his fixed toothy smile.

"That's not exactly…"

"But isn't the whole idea of the new CAT scan machine to help people? To help our great doctors better diagnose illness and injuries and better decide whether people should be sent to other places? What's the matter, aren't the workers at our local hospital good enough for you?"

"No. Not at all. Look…"

"You say that our hospital administrator and our chairman of the hospital board who also happens to be our Commonwealth's Attorney are a couple of crooks."

"I didn't say…"

"You said they 'looted' the hospital! Doesn't that make them crooks?"

"I was more…"

"You've been running around accusing some of the leading citizens in our County of being thieves and stirring up the local population against them when all they're guilty of is bringing state of the art medical technology to our local hospital! They're trying to help us and you're repaying them by calling them common criminals!"

"That machine is hardly…"

"Who told you that there is a problem with the machine? Mr. Dennis Wells? He's a trouble- maker just like you! Have you ever heard of Dr. Peter Dorman? Are you aware that he is a board- certified radiologist? Do you know that he is the staff radiologist at our local hospital? Did you know that he is a real doctor, an M.D., and not just some animal doctor, and that he finished an internship and a residency in radiology and that Dr. Dorman has said that he personally requested the CAT scan machine and that in his opinion it is the best around?"

"Now wait a minute…"

"No sir! You wait a minute! You've been destroying the reputations of some of the finest men in our society and I think you should apologize!"

"What?"

"But first a word from our sponsor!"

I stood up and started to leave. The smile was still fixed on old Brandon's face and in a stage whisper he said "Don't leave. We're not finished yet."

"Oh yes we are. Bye." And I walked out. Brandon was still smiling.

That radio show was just the first part of the Judge's campaign to repair the damage done by Butch and Al's carelessness. Every morning, Brandon Fields had a different dignitary bashing me and supporting Butch, Al and the Cat scan machine. Walter Mayhew, my nemesis on the rescue squad, even came on to say that the Squad had no problem with delaying the helicopter transports until after the Cat scan had been done. It was just me. I had "personal problems." Translated, that meant I was crazy. The newspapers were filled with articles extolling the benefits of CAT scanning while defining the proper role of volunteer rescue squads as subservient to local hospitals.

The well-orchestrated public relations campaign was working. While a few people believed that I was on the wrong side of the issue; many more were reminded that Butch and Al were the "Judge's Boys" and in Patrick County you don't mess with the Judge's boys. I was no longer popular. Nobody was slapping me on the back or shaking my hand. In fact, I was lucky if folks would talk to me or look at me at all. The parking lot at my veterinary hospital was empty and so was my waiting room. I was losing a lot of money every day and I had few cash reserves to fall back on. I was still running calls with the rescue squad but Walter Mayhew was running around telling the other members that I was a liability to the entire squad and if they were smart, they'd kick me out and elect him Captain, after all, he knew how to "get along" in Patrick County. My wife Glenda was beside herself. I had destroyed my life over a stupid volunteer job that didn't pay anything. Everything she said to me began with the phrase "You Idiot..." It was obvious that the marriage itself was on the skids.

I had become an outcast in a small county where everyone knew everyone else and where being an outcast is particularly lonely. No one wants to be seen comforting the pariah lest they join him in his lonely state. Dennis Wells, the complaining radiation technologist was fired. So were five other hospital employees who had been known to criticize the hospital. Nedra and Sylvia Baker, the accountant kept their jobs. They had been more discreet.

The best friends I had at this time were Rosalind and Andy. Their door was always open, and I was always welcome. They talked about a wide range of topics and they kept me laughing. Their support was a lifesaver. I didn't think things could get much worse. Then they did.

I was about to get into my Jeep at the end of a long un-busy day at work on a dark, rainy fall afternoon when a hand suddenly grabbed my right shoulder from behind. There was no warning. I whirled around and hit my assailant squarely in the middle of his face with my left fist. He staggered back and I hit him again, harder now, with my right fist and then again with my left. He went to the ground. I had been taught not to give

windows from floor to ceiling along an entire wall. There were bookshelves lining the other walls filled with glistening law books that obviously were ornamental and not for reading. The carpet was beige and luxurious. There was a truly massive desk and several leather wing chairs arranged before it. All around the office were various versions of "No Smoking" signs. My new attorney was in his fifties, slim, tanned with black hair and a dramatic black moustache over teeth so perfect that only expensive dentistry could have created them. He radiated intensity. After exchanging brief pleasantries, he got down to the serious business at hand. I expected him to congratulate me on my good citizenship and tell me that I had nothing to worry about. He didn't.

"You're guilty and you will lose this case in any court in the Commonwealth of Virginia."

"What about the first amendment protections of free speech?" I blurted.

"Free speech is not always free. Besides, this is no first amendment case. All that defamation and slander language in your suit is mostly nonsense. Most people decide someone is a skunk on their own and it's difficult to show damages just because you call someone a skunk. No. This case is about tortuous subversion of business practices. You are not an employee of the hospital. You are not an owner. You are not an officer of the corporation nor a member of the board of trustees. The hospital is a privately- owned corporation, and you have no standing in that corporation. Virginia law is quite clear on this subject. No matter what you might think, no matter how egregious his compensatory package may seem to you, no matter what criticisms you personally may have concerning the structure of the corporation you may not publicly comment on those feelings nor campaign to have his compensation reduced nor have him removed from his position. Put bluntly, 'no legal standing' means it's none of your damn business."

"I thought the hospital belonged to the County."

"It doesn't matter what you thought. You're in the wrong here; and sir, I have some very bad news. The law provides for the award of treble damages for this tort. You may find yourself owing Mr. Fusco $31.5 million."

"But I don't have that kind of money..."

"It doesn't matter. The Court will liquidate most of your assets and then take a large portion of your future earnings and your entire estate when you die. Unless you pay off the judgment you will belong to Mr. Fusco and his heirs and assigns forever. Around the courthouse we refer to this as a deadly lawsuit and BANG! You're dead!"

"There's got to be something we can do..."

"Sure. I'll try and hold this thing off as long as I can and introduce a bunch of motions to delay the inevitable. Then we'll use what I call the DAD: the dumbass defense. You were ignorant and stupid and in way over your head, we'll throw ourselves on the mercy of the court. You need to be prepared for a long slog. This thing could drag on for years. You'll need to spend at least an hour with me every week for a while. When I need you, you need to come when called.

"The bright side is that you have the best lawyer in the world for this type of case,

"I stood up, shook his hand and thanked him.

"Don't thank me. I'm here for the money. Thank Mr. Weston." I later learned that Mr. Weston had been billed nearly $200,000.00 for the work done by Mr. Epstein up to that point.

It was a typical fall afternoon and there was a cold steady rain falling. Rain that has such small drops, it was difficult to tell if it was really rain, or just a heavy gray mist. The sidewalks in Richmond were full of scurrying people in coats and hats many carrying umbrellas. I was in my hat, my boots and covered to the ground in a drover's coat. I stopped in the doorway of Mr. Epstein's building and lit a cheroot. I looked and felt out of place as I pushed into the crowd. I never felt more alone in my life. I was a lone cowboy from the wild west of Patrick County jostling the Friday afternoon rush hour crowds in the big city of Richmond. I had just lost a war that I didn't know I was in. It was a war that I didn't understand. A war I was ill-prepared to fight.

I drove home along Route 360 back to Highway 58. The radio was off. I was lost in my thoughts, chewing the cold cheroot and blaming myself for what apparently was my financial demise. Once in Patrick County, I went into a grocery store. There were many people in the store but none of them made eye contact with me. No one said a word to me.

When I returned to my house, it was empty. There was not a stick of furniture. Taped to the wall were some legal papers titled *A Vinculo Matrimoni*. There was a note in Glenda's handwriting which said in part

"Sign this, you son of a bitch. I can't believe you threw it all away after everything we went through."

That night we had our last little meeting at the bookstore. Andy pored over the lawsuit and essentially agreed with Mr. Epstein's assessment. I didn't want them to feel sorry for me, but I'm sure they did. Andy suggested "What we need is more information. I'm positive that these fellows have committed other, more serious crimes that we could use to blackmail them with and force them to drop this lawsuit." It was an expected response considering Andy's experience in handling difficult situations.

The meeting ended early and I followed Nedra into the street. She turned and placed the palm of her hand into the middle of my chest, pushing me away. "I'm sorry but I warned you this might happen. I just can't be seen with you until this all blows over. I'm sorry about your divorce in one way…" then suddenly she kissed me. It was a deep, fabulous kiss that left me weak in the knees. She kissed me like I had never been kissed. Then she was gone.

I got into my Jeep and drove. I meandered around the back roads of the County for a long while thinking, and becoming, more depressed. Eventually I found myself parked on a lonely stretch of road next to the Mayo River. I had a pistol. I used it to shoot horses, and cattle when there was nothing more I could do for them. It was a Colt .45 Model 1873 also known as a single action Army, the Peacemaker, the Equalizer or "the gun that won the west." It had a case-hardened finish and staghorn grips. It was a gift from a favorite uncle after I spent a high school summer working on his ranch near Alpine, Texas. The pistol had been made around the turn of the century and showed the wear and tear of a working tool. The bluing was rubbed off the barrel and the butt was chipped and dented from frequent use as a hammer to repair fences. The cylinder was out of phase so that it shaved a little lead sometimes, showering the shooter's hand with bits of hot metal. I loved that Colt and now I considered using it to blow out my brains. I was in that dark corner where people sometimes find themselves. The corner where all is lost, and hope is vanquished; where the walls of that corner are made of self-pity and depression. It requires cloudy thinking. Suicide is never the answer. It's unnatural. In the human spirit there is always hope, hope that can tear down the walls of that dark corner and set the most tortured soul free. I'm not sure how close to going through with it, but I was thinking about it.

As I looked at the beautiful old Colt I thought about my uncle. He had died the previous year. As a young man he had been drafted during his first year of college and had landed on Omaha Beach, D-Day, H-Hour. He never talked about Normandy. Others did. I was well aware of what he must have experienced. Most of his comrades had died or been severely wounded as German machine guns raked the beach. He survived unscathed, and in his words, walked to Germany. After the war, he never returned to college, but went to west Texas, married, and spent his life in the cattle business. It was never easy. He persevered. He'd never been sick a day in his life and was killed by a sudden heart attack. His life and the things he had overcome made my current troubles seem small by comparison. Perhaps his life was the source of my new-found hope.

I suppose had I shot myself, the conventional wisdom would be that it was because my wife Glenda had left me. Actually, I was happy Glenda had gone. It wasn't my failed marriage or even the lawsuit. I was sad because I didn't think this mess would ever blow over during my life. Also, I would never see Nedra again.

I slept that night in my Jeep. After all, there were no beds in my house. Glenda took 'em.

It was a Friday night and Sylvia Baker was working late adding up accounts at her desk. She nearly fainted when her chair was violently spun around and she was looking into the flashing eyes of Nedra LaPeltier. "Look, Bitch, you got him into this mess, and you've got to get him out! We need to search Fusco's files and find some real dirt on him! Now let's go! I don't care if it takes all night!"

Mr. Fusco didn't keep files in his opulent office. There was another room for that, lined with filing cabinets. There was a huge copying machine, a paper shredder and a table. The two women went to work searching through file drawers. They were about to give up when they came to a smaller locked cabinet in the corner. "I wish we could check that one." remarked Sylvia as she began to collect her things to leave. Nedra pulled out a bobby pin and in a few seconds picked the lock. Inside were folders filled with copies of checks and letters from Bermuda, the Grand

Caymans and the Bahamas. There were also deposit slips to banks in New England and New York.

"What's this stuff about?"

Sylvia took one look and said, "Sweet Jesus. It's money laundering."

They began to carefully copy all the documents. The papers were returned precisely as they found them. It was nearly dawn when they finished. Sylvia looked up at her accomplice, "Nedra, this is dangerous. People don't sue you over this type of thing. They kill you. We can't let anyone trace this back to us."

Nedra thought for a minute and said. "I'll make a plan." They collected their evidence and left just as the eastern sky was streaking with red.

The next day as Nedra outlined her plan to Sylvia, Sylvia asked, "Won't he recognize my voice?"

"Not a chance. He ain't that smart." Nedra was right.

On Wednesday morning, my secretary told me that I had a "personal" telephone call. I didn't recognize the voice of the woman on the line who said "There's a pay phone on the wall outside the drug store. Be there at nine o'clock tonight. When the phone rings, answer it." Then she hung up.

It was a cold night and under my coat I had the loaded Colt .45 in a shoulder holster. I walked up to the telephone and it rang. The same voice told me to "Stand still and don't turn around until I tell you." I expected to be shot in the back of the head as I stared at my reflection in the chrome face of the pay phone.

Meanwhile, Nedra, disguised with a baseball cap, dark glasses and a heavy coat ran across the parking lot and placed the money-laundering documents in my Jeep. After a long, long pause, the voice came back on the line. "In your Jeep is everything you need to send the bastards to jail." It was the first time in her life that Sylvia had said the word "bastards" out loud.

I hung up, turned and walked to the Jeep, driving away as fast as I could, only glancing at the four-inch thick folder on the passenger seat. I went to the Dairy Queen and under the lights flipped through the papers. I went straight to Andy and Rosalind.

As it happened there was no one better to take the papers to than Andy Pense. During his career in the Agency, Andy had developed contacts in BCCI, the huge criminal bank. At first, he used the bank to launder money for the Agency, using the funds to finance operations that not everyone would approve of. Later, he used those same contacts to completely destroy what had become the largest bank in the world when the bank's continued operation became contrary to the interests of the United States.

Andy pored over the file, smoking furiously. He looked up finally with a huge smile on his face and said "By God, Boy, you've got it! I just can't imagine why anyone would be so stupid as to allow this kind of evidence to be found or to exist, but here it is! Here it is! Good for you! It's money laundering on a huge scale. My guess is that this is Gambino money. These banks are the same ones they have used before. Rather unimaginative on their part I should think. Here's what we should do, make an appointment with your solicitor in Richmond. I'll go with you. In my opinion I'd say you're off the hook.

"Well then, let's have a drink of something…" Andy said, and we drank whatever Rosalind brought us until we were both quite drunk. It was a celebration of sorts.

A week later, Andy and I drove to Mr. Epstein's fabulous office in Richmond. Andy looked like he'd spent the night in a dumpster. His white hair was tousled sticking out in every direction with no recent evidence of a brush. He wore a navy- blue blazer that was dirty and rumpled to the point that it looked as if he had slept in it possibly for a week. His gray slacks were frayed at the cuffs and had what could have been faded grass stains on the knees. His tasseled loafers were at least one tassel short and scuffed. He had no socks. He wore a light blue shirt and a red tie that was tied in his usual off-center small tight knot. Andy gave the impression of a man who had been on a bender and was either hung over or still drunk. I shook hands with Mr. Epstein but Andy didn't grasp Mr. Epstein's offered hand. He was preoccupied with lighting a cigarette with his Zippo as he settled into one of the large leather wing chairs. I settled into the other wing chair as Andy, in defiance of all the "No Smoking" signs blew a thick cloud of smoke across the massive desk and into Mr. Epstein's now contorted face.

"Excuse me" began Epstein, "but who are you?"

"Oh. Right. Andy Pence, sir. So nice to meet you." Now Andy offered his hand and it was Epstein's turn not to shake it.

"And who exactly are you?" Earl J. Epstein was obviously becoming agitated.

"I'm a friend of your client and we have brought along some materials you may find useful to the case at hand." He handed the folder to Epstein after flicking ashes onto the posh carpet. Epstein's expression reflected absolute revulsion.

For nearly an hour Epstein read the papers, turning each page carefully, silently. I stared out the window at the skyline of Richmond. Andy fell asleep.

When he finished, the great litigator slowly closed the cover on the file and exhaled as if completely exhausted. "You need to forget about this." he began. "There is more to life than money. True, they're going to beat you up in court but maybe we can minimize the damage. Whoever is behind this" and he thumped the folder "is a dangerous individual. The type of person who makes his own law and can wreak havoc on his enemies. You don't want to be one of these enemies. This material is dangerous. Do you understand? You can lose your life just for possessing this folder.

"I suggest you completely destroy all your copies, take whatever happens in the lawsuit like a man and forget you ever saw any of this. As your attorney, that's my advice."

Andy shifted in his chair. "We're choosing to ignore your advice and directing you to forward this material to the Plaintiff's attorney at once. We don't have to take your advice, as you well know but you have to do as we direct you, unless, of course, you choose to resign in which case I would imagine you will suffer a rather significant financial penalty." Andy and I stood up and shuffled out of the office, leaving behind the folder and a thick cloud of cigarette smoke.

Back on the street, Andy did a passing imitation of Earl J. Epstein, Esq. "Whoever is behind this is a dangerous individual. Do you understand? You can lose your life."

Andy suddenly stopped laughing and became as serious as I had ever seen him. He opened his blue blazer to reveal a Walther PPK automatic pistol in a fine shoulder holster. He spoke in his British accent. "Fuck'em if they can't take a joke."

The following Friday afternoon, Mr. Fusco dropped his lawsuit against me without comment. Once again, I was a popular figure. I was Jack the Giant slayer. No one knew exactly how I had done it, but I had won.

Rosalind made it plain that if I said a word to the press, she would never speak to me again.

As a newly divorced man I invited Nedra out to dinner in Mt. Airy. We laughed and talked as never before. There wasn't the tension that had been there before. On the way home, she pointed to a motel and said "… pull in here." I did. That night we became lovers.

Early the next morning, a large gleaming black Cadillac with three well-dressed men arrived unannounced at Mr. Al Fusco's house. The head honcho informed Al that he was to be assigned to a hospital in New Orleans and he was to go with them. They'd come back for his things later. As Fusco packed a bag he was elated. Wherever he was going, it had to be better than Hillbilly Land. He loved New Orleans. They didn't mention it to Al, but the three men were members of the Marcello organization, the Louisiana crime family. A family known as enforcers to the mob.

They drove all day and through the night arriving early in the morning at a deserted dock where there was a waiting air boat. "The bosses want to meet with you" said the leader and the air boat took off deep into the swamps of Louisiana. At their destination, there were no bosses, just an old barge with a large rusty wood -chipper on it and five tough-looking men in coveralls. With no ceremony or discussion, they fed Mr. Alfonse Fusco wearing his Italian shoes and his Armani suit feet first and alive into the wood- chipper. The Adonis, the Greek God ended up as a pink mist over a deserted bayou. The larger bits were eaten by little fish as they drifted down into the black water. The pieces missed by the fish were consumed by crawfish when they came to rest on the muddy bottom. The kick of the pony had been lethal.

An auction company from Danville sold Fusco's house and possessions for pennies on the dollar so that in two weeks, it was as if Mr. Al Fusco had never existed in the county. As if he had never existed in the world.

The sudden, complete disappearance of his erstwhile partner was frightening to Butch Russell. His sleep was broken by visions of grisly murder. His own murder. He packed a suitcase with cash and went straight to his father-in-law's car dealership and traded his big new white Lincoln for a used Buick. Then he headed south, finally checking into a quiet hotel in Roxboro, North Carolina under a false name. Butch Russell was hiding.

"Doc! Doc!" called Maggie. "Here. You stick this vein. My hands are shaking too much." That made my stomach hurt. I sure didn't want to be the guy to bugger a vein on this lady. I started to ask Nedra for help, but since the bleeding in the shoulder was somewhat controlled, she was busy helping Larry Cane and Jarrell Price put an E-Collar and a KED board on Kathy. Sometimes, in certain situations the trick is not to think too much. As Maggie and Rusty extended the pale white arm, I slid the long stainless- steel needle covered by its Teflon catheter straight into the vein. I was hyperventilating when I saw the rich red blood pour out of the hub. I slid the needle out and began taping the catheter in place. Maggie released the tourniquet and I hooked up the Lactated Ringers. The flow rate for the fluids was set at "W.O" for "Wide Open."

In seconds, we were lifting Mrs. Kathy Bragg out of her ruined car and securing her to a long wooden backboard. She was put on high flow Oxygen as the ambulance rushed to the hospital with full lights and sirens. The helicopter was already in route.

Suddenly, with the JEB Stuart crew gone, I felt alone, the area seemed strangely quiet. There was no talking, just the sound of the generator for the lights and the sounds of firemen picking up debris and washing off the roadway. I saw Myron Pappas sitting by himself on the side of a bank. He was staring at the wreckage. "Is he all right?" I asked a passing fireman.

"Yeah, just tore up. He said that he saw another car but now he's not so sure and he's afraid he hallucinated. Keeps telling us how sorry he is. He signed off on transport and treatment."

"Any other victims?"

"Just the fatality. I don't think you can do much for him, though."

"Thanks."

"Sure." And the fireman moved off into the darkness. For the first time I turned my attention to the passenger in the car. For some reason, the corpse had not been covered with a sheet. Also, I saw Nedra. She was smeared with blood and was standing stock still staring at the dead man. She looked drained. It occurred to me that while she frequently saw horrible things in the E.R., she may not have been prepared for the macabre scenes of death that were routinely encountered by rescue squads in the field.

The headless body was slumped against the closed door. There was little blood on the white dress shirt. The right hand was in the man's lap and the left hand hung over the door where the window would have been. Instead of a head there was a large crimson wound. A portion of the rear of the skull was still attached to the neck but no brain material was visible. The floor of the brain compartment and the nasal sinuses were clearly identifiable. A large piece of scalp was neatly rolled up over the collar of the white shirt. It was as if the head had been prepared as an anatomy specimen by sawing the skull off just above the mouth.

I walked slowly over to Nedra and as gently as I could, I lightly touched her shoulder. She didn't move. She was staring at the gruesome thing in the car and then she spoke quietly, "He's still holding his cigar." Now I noticed that between the left index finger and middle finger was a large brown cigar. It was no longer lit.

Had the Tutterow's been successful with their attempt at shooting me in the head with a high-powered rifle, I might well have wound up looking like the late Mr. Lewis E. Bragg. We never know what the future holds and none of us have a guarantee that there will be a tomorrow.

While Nedra and I were heading home in my Jeep to a shared shower and lovemaking; the Judge in his study stared through his window at nothing but darkness. "If you want something done, you have to do it yourself." he thought. There were those who had to be punished; to be taught a lesson and The Judge would do the teaching himself. The legal war fought with lawyers as surrogates was over. A new type of war was beginning. A violent, deadly war.

if anyone ever found out about the strange relationship, he would fight them in court and the monetary payments would stop. So, as the girl grew into a female version of her father, only four people knew the truth with certainty: Stella, her mother, the Judge and the child herself: Mary Dell Oates.

As the little girl grew, the visits by her father became more frequent and he began to give her advice which basically consisted of aiming high by working hard on her education. Mary Dell was not especially talented, but she did work diligently to compensate and was rewarded by staying at the top of her class. The Judge made sure that she attended the best private schools and received tutoring when necessary. It was not a happy childhood. There were no activities outside her studies. She was known as a quiet, sad girl who with her bird-like features was never considered a beauty. She never called the Judge "Papa," or "Daddy" or "Father." She called him "The Judge."

Her mother and grandmother imbued her with a distrust for all men. From her earliest life, she was told to stay away from men, all men, and to never wind up in a position of depending on a man for anything. Somehow a woman had to be able to fend for herself and build a life free of any man.

The little girl worked with grim determination to claw her way up the academic ladder, graduating as her high school's valedictorian. Combined with high test scores and the Judge's money she could attend any college she chose. She chose the University of Virginia, where she continued to excel in academia, but the sad, lonely young lady had no friends. There had been no question but that she should study law and when the time came, she went to Yale.

After graduation, she easily passed the Virginia Bar exam and entered private practice with a large firm in Martinsville. Within a year, she became an assistant prosecutor in the Office of the Commonwealth's Attorney. Putting bad men in prison was much more rewarding than writing up deeds probating wills and handling contracts. She became an expert in criminal law and a force that Henry County defense attorneys learned to respect. But it wasn't enough. Hidden beneath the patina of the shy, hardworking woman was an intense ambition fed by the Judge's exhortations to aim high in life. Truly her mother's daughter, there were no men in her life, but, thanks to the Judge's continued cash payments, she enjoyed a comfortable lifestyle with an expensive condominium, fashionably conservative clothes, the best shoes and adequate spa time. She bought a new car every year, ate at the best restaurants and went to events with the best tickets. Once a year she took a fabulous vacation by herself.

When an opening occurred at the U. S. Attorney's office in Roanoke, she applied for it and was hired. The Judge had said that the Commonwealth's Attorney's office in Henry County was a "backwater" and she should serve as a U.S. Attorney and then run for elective office, perhaps State Attorney General or Lieutenant Governor. She would then be positioned to be Governor and from there, who knows? Perhaps high federal office, either appointed or elected.

One afternoon, the Judge appeared in her Roanoke office. He told her that there should be no federal investigation of certain events in Patrick County involving the hospital. That was all he said. He left an envelope containing a large amount of cash on her desk. He then stalked out the door without saying goodbye.

Two weeks later, the Judge was back in her office. This time he was more dour than usual. His face was even paler than usual and the wrinkles around his eyes were deeper than usual.

"I am sorry that I have to ask you to do this thing for me, but I have no choice." He spoke without emotion in his voice as he fixed her in the cross-eyed chicken stare. In some ways the old heron was again looking at a frog or a fish, but there was something different this time: a sense of desperation. The old heron knew the end was near. He knew he was weakened. The years of fighting battles and winning had taken a toll. Now he saw new battles ahead and was not at all certain he could fight them; much less win.

"There are three people that need to be removed. They potentially could bring me down-destroy everything I've worked for and done over my entire lifetime." Now the Judge was staring back through the years. "I won't be criminally charged and tried of course. If it comes to that, I'll shoot myself first, but don't think you're not involved. My existence and my power is essential to your continued success. You very much stand on my shoulders as you reach for the heavens, and if I fall, so do you. Also, there may be a thorough investigation of my finances including the meticulous records I've kept on cash contributions made to you. My guess would be that you have neither reported them as gifts nor as straight income. I would have done the same in your situation. But, you are vulnerable to criminal prosecution by the IRS.

"Here are enough resources to easily accomplish what I want done." With that the Judge opened a brown leather brief case on her desk. "There is $200,000.00 here. You may need it all to get the job done, but when it's successfully completed, I will transfer one million dollars to you in any manner you wish. I will also publicly admit my relationship to you. At least it will make your bastardry more dignified.

"Here is all the information you should require." The Judge pulled a large envelope from his coat. It contained photographs and personal information on Nedra, Druisilla and me. "We've been using members of the Pagans or Outlaws for this type of work in the past. Find one in your custody and help gain his release. That will establish his trust in you. He'll appreciate freedom more than money. Then you pay him a large sum of money now and more later when he does the job. Now, it is important that the one you have contact with not actually perform the task. Your contact must not be directly implicated, since he could lead back to you. Tell him to hire another party and he must be instructed never to use your name. After the work is done, you must tell him to eliminate the third party. I'll then see that the one you hired is also removed and we will have adequately protected ourselves. Tell him it is a favor for New York Interests. He should understand."

With that the Judge left. A sitting Judge had just blackmailed her, his own daughter no less, to arrange a triple homicide. She had never signed on for this and the Dell side of her had a conscience and a sense of fear. The Assistant U. S. Attorney, Mary Dell Oates, reached for her trash can and vomited into it.

The following day, she asked her secretary if there were any members of Outlaw Motorcycle Gangs in federal custody. Right away the secretary replied, "There's that guy in Martinsville who nearly killed a federal witness on a drug case Russ Jeffers was handling. He's a Pagan or something. Haven't you seen the news articles on it? Anyway, Russ decided to let the Henry County C. A.'s office handle it since it was in their jurisdiction and Russ didn't have time to prosecute a major case."

Mary Dell Oates got the file and read it. When she was finished, she whispered to herself, "Perfect."

That afternoon, Gail Wilson took a call from the U. S. Attorney's Office in Roanoke. "Gail? Mary. Listen, I'm taking over the Randy McAllen case. Myers was our guy and it really pisses me off that McAllen tried to kill him. We've got other federal charges we can bring, and I think I can get him put away forever. You know as well as I do that in the state system, this guy might get released someday. I don't want that asshole on the street ever again."

"But Mary, I've got a lot done on this case already." Replied Gail. "I've interviewed some great witnesses. I can put him away and if Myers dies, I've got a shot at the death penalty. I'm not going to fight you over this…I can't fight you over this…but Mary, please consider…"

"I'll send my associate down there tomorrow to get your files. We'll take care of the paperwork." And with that, Mary Dell Oates hung up. Randy McAllen's case became federal.

Randy McAllen was taken in handcuffs from his cell at the Martinsville jail to a small interview room. He asked to have the handcuffs removed so he could smoke, and he reached into his shirt pocket fumbling for a pack of cigarettes. Seated at the table was a not unattractive woman in a fashionable suit with unmanaged black hair, wide eyes and a sharp beak-like nose. She was obviously all business. She was not there for fun and games. In violation of jail rules, there was no officer in the room. The two of them were alone. The curtains were drawn over the two-way mirror and the cameras and other recording devices had been removed.

The woman leaned toward Randy across the table and spoke in a quiet but intense voice. "I can squash you like a cockroach and you could rot for the rest of your miserable life in jail. It would be easy for me." began Mary Dell Oates, the U.S. Attorney.

"Do I need my lawyer here?" asked Randy.

"Not if you want to get out of this mess. I'm the only person in this whole wide world who can help you. I'm your only chance. You understand that?" Randy nodded. "Nothing in this world is free. If I get you out, you need to do something for me, and you better not fuck with me because I will have you tracked down and killed in a horrible way. Do you understand me?" Again, Randy nodded. She asked Randy if he knew

I showed the two Pagans into my office and as I went behind my desk, I caught a glimpse of the unmistakable walnut grip of a Smith and Wesson .357 magnum nickel-plated revolver in a shoulder holster. The "drug dealer special," it was called. In an open, top desk drawer I kept my service automatic, a model 1911-A Colt Combat Commander with a brushed nickel finish. In one quick motion I pulled the pistol out of the drawer and worked the slide action chambering a round. Holding the weapon in two hands I pointed it first at one then the other of the two Pagans. "Put your hands up."

They raised their hands slowly then looked at each other and began to laugh. Randy pointed his finger at me, "You got it man. You got the right idea all right! Yeah man, They're tryin' to kill your ass. In fact, a goddam U. S. Attorney has taken a hit out on you. A goddam U. S. Attorney! They're just one step down from God Almighty. I been in a lot of jackpots but I never had a U. S. Attorney take a contract out on me. You must have really fucked up. Well, uh, look here Dog, we ain't here to do anything to you so, if you don't mind, how 'bout you uncock that thing so we can talk." I did and they lowered their hands. "The guy that you gotta watch for" continued Randy, "is one ugly son of a bitch. Tall, skinny, real white skinned, almost bald. Name of Herman Hulce. Drives a big white '68 Caddy that he keeps highly polished. Virginia plates XDU 4338. Confederate flag sticker on the rear window. He hangs out at a place in Danville called the Double Duce. He's a crazy-dangerous mother fucker. He's supposed to get your girlfriend and her daughter too. I don't think I'd go to the law. They're the ones that are after you." He looked at the Colt pistol still in my hand. "You might ought to handle it yourself and I hope you fuck the bastard up." With that, the two pagans got up and left my office, but Randy turned as he walked out the door. "We're even. You and me." It was the last time I ever saw him.

I took the information directly to Andy. In two days, he presented me with the long criminal record of Herman Frederick Hulce. Andy had the contacts and his stock and trade was information. He frowned as he talked about Mr. Hulce. "This is potentially a bad situation for you, and I do hope you'll be vigilant. I don't think this is coming from the Gambino's. They would never risk hiring someone so, let's say, unpredictable as our friend Mr. Hulce. More than likely this is coming from the local bad boys. We may have to wait for him to make a move or we could strike first. Risky business, but necessary. Let me research this a bit and I'll come up with a plan. Meanwhile, you will be careful, won't you?"

I looked at the long list of arrests and convictions of Mr. Herman Frederick Hulce. Most involved assaults and robberies but one entry caught my eye. Herman Hulce had been charged in 1978 with the rape assault of Miss Michelle Frazier in Stokes County North Carolina. Miss Frazier had worked as a bank teller. One afternoon, she left work and didn't make it home. The next morning, some hunters had found her naked, unconscious and all but dead on a logging road in the back country. Her head injuries were so severe that she never again spoke coherently and was unable to participate in the investigation. Witnesses had identified Herman Hulce as the man seen walking up to her in the parking lot that fateful day. Semen matched Herman's blood type in those pre-DNA days and Herman had several sexual assaults in his record. It would have been enough for a conviction, but his landlady testified that Herman and the victim had had a secret love affair and Hulce had entertained her that night at his house. The landlady added that Michelle had left in her own car which was found later near the scene and the jury failed to arrive at a guilty verdict. The landlady's testimony was enough for reasonable doubt, especially in the absence of other evidence.

I knew Michelle Frazier. We had been classmates in high school. We had been on the school newspaper staff together. Michelle was the cartoonist. We had never been close friends and I'd lost track of her, but as I read the record, I saw the pretty, smiling face of the happy artistic girl I had known. Oh yeah, I would take care of Mr. Herman Frederick Hulce.

Andy and Rosalind had to go to a dinner party at Dr. Arthur Phillips' home, so I went home and stuck the .45 Colt with the staghorn grips under the mattress on my side of the bed. I thought about warning Nedra but I knew she would leave and a snake like Hulce would just find her later. This way, using the people I loved as bait, I had a chance of taking care of Mr. Hulce permanently.

One morning the mail clerk wheeled his cart into the office of Mary Dell Oates, and deposited the neat little stack of letters and two magazines on her desk. There was also a small package wrapped in plain brown paper which could have been made from a paper bag. The address was scrawled in black crayon. There was no return address. At first, Mary Dell's secretary considered sending the package down to security for examination, X-Ray and opening, but Mary Dell hurriedly collected all her mail and took it into her inner office where she opened the small package first. It was a small cassette player/recorder with a cassette in it. Mary Dell pressed PLAY.

The recording was scratchy and poor quality. There were sounds of breathing and the rubbing of fabric over the microphone, but then a voice could be heard. The voice was distant and difficult to hear but it could be heard well enough. It was the voice of Mary Dell Oates. "I could squash you like a cockroach and you could rot for the rest of your miserable life in jail. It would be…" Mary Dell pressed STOP. She had heard enough. She was sure the entire incriminating conversation between her and Randy McAllen was on that tape. For the first time she noticed a brief handwritten note, printed in crayon.

> *There is six copies of this tape. If somthing (sic) hapens (sic)*
> *to me or to Mr. Hulce, then my freind (sic) will send copy*
> *to newspapers and judges and other important people.*
> *Don't fuck with me.*

The ordered safe life of Mary Dell Oates was out of control. She vomited into the trash can. As she wiped her mouth, she wondered how she should go about killing that asshole.

But it was too late. Randy McAllen had loaded a large rental truck with his favorite motorcycles and a large amount of cash. After that, he disappeared into America.

Mr. Ray Edward (Hop-a-Long) Meyers also disappeared. In 2003, some bones were found inside a dry well in Horsepasture, Virginia. There were a couple of well-worn long bones and remnants of a mandible with a few teeth in it. The tibia that was found was deformed by an apparent congenital defect. Had anyone known whom to compare the bones to, DNA from the teeth would have matched Hop-a-Long, but as it was there was no matching report of a missing person and no one came forward to claim the remains. Since the location and condition of the bones suggested foul play, the bones were placed in a small sealed plastic container and relegated to a shelf in the Henry County evidence room. The remains would never be identified, and no further investigation occurred. A more energetic investigation might have found buried in the dust at the bottom of the dry well a ball of lead, a forty-five caliber ball of lead which would have matched the Colt Model 1911 automatic pistol that so many years before, Randy McAllen had tucked into my boot during his extrication from a wrecked car at the Spoon Creek Bridge.

M. Engle 2015

Mary Dell Oates
U.S. Attorney

CHAPTER ELEVEN

The Vice and the Price

But Arthur didn't leap to his feet. He didn't scream out. Instead, Andy Pence fell face down dead into his bowl of salad. Not dying, but dead.

Dr. Phillips jumped up and checked Andy for breathing and a pulse. Nothing. Quickly with Rosalind's assistance, Andy was lowered to the floor where Rosalind and Dr. Phillips began CPR.

"One-and-two-and-three-and-four-and-breathe-and-one-and-two-and-three-and-four- and…" counted the Mouse as he performed chest compressions. Every time he said "breathe" Rosalind administered two large rescue breaths. Mildred called the Rescue Squad. As Dr. Arthur Phillips worked, bitter tears rolled down his cheeks. He knew the CPR would do no good because he had mixed 500 milligrams of Digitalis, a heart drug derived from the foxglove plant into Andy's "special" salad dressing. At that dose, digitalis is lethal and irreversible. Phillips also knew that even if Digitalis were detected in a postmortem tox screen, Dr. Phillips himself had prescribed it to Andy for years to treat his heart disease. The presence of Digitalis would raise no red flags.

JEB Stuart arrived in minutes. Jarrell Price, Maggie Engel, Carolyn Miller and Earl Ashe ran the call. They came rushing into the house with a crash towing a cot piled high with a junk box, a drug box and an oxygen tank. With little talking, Jarrell and Carolyn established an IV catheter and line while Maggie performed a quick examination. There was no detectable pulse, no detectable breathing and the pupils were equal, dilated and fixed. That is, when a pen light was shone into the large open pupils, they didn't contract at all. It's a condition referred to informally as "blown pupils." It's a sign of death.

With a long-bladed laryngoscope Maggie Engel smoothly inserted an endotracheal tube through the larynx and into the windpipe or trachea. Earl Ashe attached the Ambu bag and began breathing for the patient while Maggie hooked up a high flow oxygen line to the bag. Carolyn made sure there was a wide open flow from the Lactated Ringers bag into the vein. Jarrell took over the chest compressions. After checking with Dr. Phillips, Maggie gave first an I.V. dose of epinephrine followed by a D-50 (50% Dextrose) push. As Maggie took over the bagging, Earl positioned the CPR Board on the cot, to provide a hard surface to push down on during CPR. For an instant, everyone stopped and helped move Andy onto the cot. The bagging and chest compressions were immediately resumed, but the cot was already moving toward the ambulance. Earl jumped into the driver's seat while the rest of the crew climbed into the back with Andy. Together they worked the Code (for "Code Blue", an unresponsive, non-breathing patient with no detectable pulse requiring constant CPR during transport) as the ambulance raced to the hospital with lights and siren. During the trip, Andy made no motion. He didn't breathe a single gasp. There was never a detectable pulse and the pupils were blown.

Rosalind and Dr. and Mrs. Phillips followed the ambulance in Arthur's Mercedes to the hospital. None of the three spoke a single word during the trip.

Dr. Wayne Toms was the emergency room physician that night. Nedra was also on duty. Maggie Engel had already contacted the hospital and told them what was happening. The emergency room staff was ready. Andy was placed on the cardiac bed. High flow oxygen and chest compressions were continued. Andy was connected to an EKG machine. The tracing was a continuous flat straight line. Cardiac a systole it's called. No electrical activity in the heart. In the nature of a "Hail Mary" gesture, Dr. Toms shocked Andy three times with the paddles in a desperate effort to restart the heart. At the same time, Nedra was administering the drug protocol for cardiac arrest. Nothing worked. As a last effort, Toms gave an injection of epinephrine directly into the heart.

At 9:32 p.m. Mr. Andrew Ewell Pense, age 62, was pronounced dead. In life he had been a scholar, a Marine veteran of the Korean War, and a hero in the covert wars fought between the Capitalist West and the Communist East. He was the dedicated husband of Rosalind, a book store owner, and the savior of the Patrick County hospital. He was the best friend I ever had. The death was ruled to be due to natural causes, specifically sudden cardiac arrest due to chronic heart disease. It was, in fact, a massive overdose of Digitalis. The Digitalis caused the heart to contract into a clench-fist: unresponsive to drugs, unresponsive to chest compressions, unresponsive to electricity. That dose of Digitalis hidden in the salad dressing prepared by Dr. Arthur Phillips was lethal and irreversible.

In the hallway of the E.R., Maggie Engel told Carolyn Miller that she did a good job on the call. Carolyn responded that she felt they did everything possible. "I really admire you, Maggie." Continued Carolyn. "You're so smart and you seem to have it together better than anyone."

"No, no. You just don't know." Said Maggie. "I don't have it together at all especially when someone dies." The two women were now weeping in each other's arms. With that embrace they became friends.

Nedra called me and gave me the bad news. Then she took Rosalind back to the bookstore and stayed with her for several hours. Nedra said that Rosalind comforted her more than the other way around. She could not believe how strong and brave Rosalind was in the face of such a horrible loss. When I arrived at the bookstore, Rosalind offered me some hot tea laced with rum. Soon, we were all talking about Andy as if he was coming through the door any minute. Finally, after midnight, Rosalind asked that we leave. She said she was tired and needed her sleep, but I suspect it was more out of concern for Nedra and me. She didn't want to deprive us of sleep nor burden us with her grief.

The funeral was held four days later, on a blustery clear December afternoon. There were about twenty odd mourners. We followed the hearse to Patrick Memorial Gardens for the burial. As we gathered, hunched against the cold, a caravan of black SUV's with blue and red lights flashing in their grills pulled up. A young man in a business suit opened the rear door of the third SUV and out stepped an immediately recognizable figure. There was a gasp from the other mourners as they realized the new addition to the group was George H. W. Bush, the President of the United States and a friend of Andy Pense. The President was a lame duck having been defeated in his quest for a second term by Bill Clinton only a month earlier. The President stood reverently and quietly during the brief ceremony surrounded by other young men in business suits. After the burial, the President shook hands and offered condolences to each mourner. He hugged and kissed Rosalind. When I shook hands with the President who seemed thinner and taller than I expected he said in his familiar voice, "We lost a good man."

"Yes Sir." I replied. "He voted for you. Both times." It was a stupid thing to say, I suppose, but the President was gracious enough to smile and nod his head. After only a few minutes, the motorcade disappeared back to the Danville airport. This visit by a sitting President of the United States to Patrick County was never reported in the press.

On the day before Christmas Eve, Dr. Arthur Phillips locked himself in one of the courtesy rooms used by emergency room physicians for catching some sleep during their shifts. He started an intravenous drip into his arm, beggining a slow drip of Lactated Ringers Solution with 40 Grams of Sodium Pentathol added. Death came quietly and painlessly. He left a long hand-written suicide note in which he fully admitted to killing his best friend, Andy Pence. He couldn't live with his crime he wrote, and he apologized to Rosalind. He left all of his worldly assets to his wife, Mildred.

In his note, Dr. Phillips failed to mention his gay life- style, nor that he was blackmailed by the Judge. The Judge had ordered the killing of Andy Pence for his role in bringing down the money laundering operation at the local hospital. In fact, in his note, Dr. Phillips gave no motive at all for poisoning his friend. Even in death, the Mouse was a coward. Too frightened to reveal his sexual orientation lest he hurt his family or his own reputation. Better to be a murderer. Better to horribly betray a life-long friend than to have people find out you are different. The tragedy is that even in conservative Patrick County as more and more gays identified themselves in the community, sexual orientation lost its scandalous power within the next ten years, but the real tragedy was that Arthur's cowardice and failure to implicate the Judge cost poor Andy the justice he deserved.

Rosalind for her part would see that some justice was done. She had no doubt that the Judge was behind Andy's death. She spent hours chain smoking, drinking small glasses of Scotch neat and organizing the notes from John Powers and Monk Fisher to resemble actual transcripts of tape recordings. She then contacted one of her ex-husbands. He had left the movie business and went into politics where his talents were much more appreciated. In fact, he held a high elective office in Virginia. Within a month, the Judge received a letter from an old acquaintance who was the Chief Justice of the Supreme Court of Virginia.

The letter included copies of over one-hundred and fifty pages of the manufactured transcripts. The documents implicated the Judge in the running of a criminal enterprise that spanned fifty years. It was all there except the money laundering. The Chief's letter went on to say that in light of the Judge's age, his years of faithful service on the bench and the difficulty involved in such an enormous prosecution, if the Judge resigned immediately no other action would be taken against him and the transcripts would be sealed.

As he read and reread the papers, the Judge suffered a stroke and lost the use of the right side of his body.

He still had his mental faculties and he blamed me for his situation, He could rely on Mary Dell Oates, his daughter and a sitting U. S. Attorney. She'd get his revenge. Revenge for the now wounded old heron lying in the mud at the edge of the water surrounded by reeds. The Judge was an exhausted old bird who had begun the long process of death.

President
George H. W. Bush
December, 1992

CHAPTER TWELVE

The Evil That Men Do...

We are born to love. We are taught to hate. When Herman Frederick Hulce was born on a cold February night in 1954 at a hospital in southern Indiana, he was a truly loving, normal baby. In time, he learned to hate.

The teaching began with his father, a lawyer by the name of Edwin Lane Hulce. Edwin inspected the newborn boy as one might inspect a new puppy, rolling him over and counting his fingers and toes. Having established that the baby wasn't a cull, he took his child and his mousy wife home. A home in which Edwin L. Hulce, Esq. was the authoritarian master.

Edwin's parents had been German immigrants to America who originally settled in New York, but anti-German sentiment during the First World War prompted the Hulce family to relocate to Mooresville, Indiana where the elder Hulce joined his brother in a meat-packing business that became quite successful. Successful enough to send Edwin to college and law school during the Great Depression. Southern Indiana was particularly hard hit during the Depression, and accordingly the price of pigs was very low. In fact, you were lucky if you could sell a pig at all. With so many people out of work, labor was also cheap, so the Hulce brothers bought whole pigs of any type or size and paid workers a pittance to grind them up into sausage. It wasn't the best sausage in the world, but it was cheap, and people had to eat.

The entire Hulce family had a basic belief, a creed, if you will: white people are better than other people, and German white people are better than other white people. A heart murmur fortuitously discovered by the family doctor, won a 4-F draft classification for young Edwin, keeping him out of World War II which was just as well since Edwin had no desire to fight the Germans nor their allies, the Japanese. In fact, the Hulce family felt that America was on the wrong side and should have joined Hitler instead of fighting him, but then, they believed that Roosevelt was a dupe of the world Jewish community.

Most of southern Indiana was rural with scattered small towns and a sparse population. Mooresville had been the childhood home of John if they did, were unlikely to hurt him. Herman Hulce quit picking on those his own size, instead he went after small children and girls. He also found that the elderly or handicapped were easily pushed, shoved and insulted with the only response being glares from his victims. Disapproving looks didn't hurt. They didn't swell your eyes shut or bloody your nose. By the time he was sixteen Herman Hulce was well on his way to becoming a truly despicable human being with little redeeming social value.

Public school was out of the question. Too many students of color. Edwin sent his proud son to an elite private boarding school in northern Virginia. It was a school where the ability of the family to pay the outrageous tuition was the over-riding consideration for admission and promotion. Herman found a small (very small) group of like-minded boys. The early 1970's were a time of political unrest and social upheaval in the United States. These boys, filled with hate beyond their years, fed on each other and dreamed of a new civil war which would purge the country of "others" establishing once and for all the dominance of superior members of society. Of course, these boys placed themselves within that superior group. They were sure of it. They were, after all, the little princes in their private school. Barely into adult life these scamps were certain of their distorted views of the world; the certitude that comes from lack of experience. Then, life and the world changed for Herman Hulce.

On a January night during Herman's junior year in high school, his father came home, hung his coat in the closet and promptly dropped dead in the hallway of a massive heart attack. While the family had enjoyed a well-to-do lifestyle, it had been dependent on Edwin's continuing employment. They had been living from substantial paycheck to substantial paycheck and there was little money set aside as either cash or investments. Mrs. Hulce went down the drain with the finances. She took a job at a convenience store which barely covered her own newly-modest living standards. The large, heavily mortgaged house was lost. There were no more tuition payments. Herman Hulce left school. He would never return to school anywhere. He was on his own. His only inheritance from his father was the shiny large white 1969 Cadillac two door sedan.

With little formal education, Herman went through a series of menial jobs mostly in construction. Herman's high opinion of himself and his feelings of superiority over his co-workers led to frictions in the work place. He was frequently fired. But he did find some friends: other racists who spent their spare time drinking, expounding on the sorry state of the world and shooting guns. Most of the drinking went on in a small bar in a Danville shopping center: *The Double Duce*. He took on the habit of wearing military style clothing, fatigues, camouflage and heavy boots though he had no service in the military himself. He found another habit: alcohol. Herman never used any illegal drugs (that was for the "others") but he drank prodigious amounts of beer and sometimes whiskey.

One of his new friends showed Herman how to supplement his meager income by selling marijuana and methamphetamine to the inferior types. He could make money and poison the inferiors at the same time. Later he would sell crack. Whenever he got caught, he would readily turn on his customers and associates, becoming an informant. He felt no loyalty to his drug-world associates whom he considered weak and inferior. They got what they deserved and he avoided long prison sentences.

So, in his mid-twenties, Herman Hulce, a menial laborer, and small-time drug dealer, and a young man best described as a "punk white supremacist" went into bank in Winston-Salem. He was there to cash a paycheck. The teller was Michelle Frazier, my high school classmate. Michelle was petite, with the brown eyes of a doe, long brown hair and a truly beautiful smile. It was part of her job to be friendly to customers, for Michelle it was never a chore. It came naturally. For some evil reason, Michelle's friendliness set off a spark in Herman Hulce's mind. He wanted her and not in any normal way that young men are attracted to young ladies. He wanted her and he would have her. Now.

Herman hung around the parking lot swilling beer and watching the small bank until closing time. Soon enough, Michelle appeared and walked to her car, never thinking that danger could be so close. As she opened her car door, Herman suddenly pushed her inside and demanded the car keys. She complied, and thought at first she may be involved in a bank robbery of some kind. He gripped her delicate wrist tightly with his right hand as he drove with his left. She would be all right, he promised, if she did exactly what he told her to do, otherwise, he would kill her.

Actually, Herman had no idea what to do, so he drove around the back roads, drinking and ignoring his captive, demanding that she sit close to him, and that she not move. His long thin powerful right arm was wrapped

Ronnie said as he was starting the engine of his car. He had been at my house for less than five minutes.

Late the following afternoon, I was painting over the spray-painted words on the road in front of my house with black paint. Hateful words, no matter how badly misspelled are hateful words. I heard a car approaching but I didn't look up. I just stepped out of the road. The car slowed to a crawl and as I turned to see, I was struck on the head with an empty can of white spray paint. It was a shiny white old model Cadillac and leaning out the window was Herman Hulce. It was the first time I laid eyes on him. His skin was a strange shade of pale white. His face thin and expressionless, but I was transfixed by his eyes. His eyes were large for his face and pale blue. They were soul-less. These were dead eyes. The eyes of a snake or a corpse. We stared at each other as he cruised slowly past, neither of us acknowledging the presence of the other. After a long minute, he sped up and drove away, still staring at me. A chill went through my body. A deep chill down to the bones. The Grim Reaper had driven past my house in an old shiny white Cadillac and we had stared at each other. I was afraid. Not for myself, but for Nedra and Dru. I'd have to tell Nedra.

Nedra and Dru came home after her shift about half-past midnight. As usual, Dru had fallen asleep at her grandmother's house. I carried the sleeping child into the house and tucked her in bed.

"We need to talk. Something's come up." I began.

Nedra was already taking off her clothes. "Not now, Baby. I'm tired. Let's go to bed and we'll talk some other time. I just want some fast lovin' and some slow sleepin'. We got time to talk later." She pulled me into the bedroom. But we would never have that time to talk. Herman Hulce didn't give us time.

Two hours later, something woke me, and I lay there in bed motionless, ears pricked listening. In that old frame house, the floor creaked and now I heard the floor creak. It was unmistakable. A low shallow groan followed by another. Someone was creeping down the hall. The noise of the floor told me it was an adult. Dru usually didn't make the floor creak with every step. She was too light weight. I touched Nedra. She was beside me and sound asleep. The creaky footsteps were getting closer to the open bedroom door. It had to be Herman Hulce!

Silently I pulled my uncle's Colt .45 from under the mattress. The colt is a single action revolver which means, you have to pull back the hammer with your thumb before you can fire the pistol by squeezing the trigger. The hammer, has to be in full-cock position before the gun can be fired and to pull the hammer back to the full cock position results in three distinct metallic clicks. In a silent house, those three clicks would be loud and would tip off the creeper in the hall that I was armed and ready to shoot. I'd have to wait until the last second and pull the hammer back and shoot at the same time. The un-cocked hammer interferes with aiming a bit, but this was a point and shoot situation anyway.

There was a night light in the hall that gave off an eerie yellow glow. I was sitting up now holding the pistol in both hands and pointing it towards the open bedroom door. With each creak of a floorboard my hair stood on end and the skin of my neck tingled. Suddenly there he was! The dark shape of a man and the unmistakable shape of an MP-40 in his hands. "Son of a Bitch! He's got a *machine gun!*" flashed through my mind and I fired the Colt pistol. It sounded like a cannon in that quiet dark house and a red fireball rolled across the bedroom. I leapt out of bed buck naked giving chase. Nedra and Druisilla were both screaming. I got into the hall and saw the dark shape running through the kitchen; out the back door. I fired again. Now I was running after him. I was holding an antique pistol with three rounds left to fire and chasing a man with a machine gun. If he turned and cut me in half with that machine gun, I might get one shot, one chance to put a .45 slug right between his eyes which to me in that time and place would be well worth it.

But I couldn't catch him. He had fled across the yard and into the surrounding woods. He knew where he was going, and I didn't. I fired another shot into the woods, not with any hope of finding a target, but out of anger and frustration. A parting shot to send him on his way. A warning not to come back. In the still distance, I heard a car drive off.

I just had time to put on some pants before the deputies arrived. Nedra had called them and soon the yard was filled with flashing blue lights. Deputy Ronnie Branch interviewed me. I told him what had happened. He winced at my story and asked if I was sure there was something really there? Could it be that I was just spooked by the cross burning and word-painting of the previous night? Could it be that I just imagined a machine-gun toting boogie man in my hall? Could it be that I was shooting at shadows? Well, yeah. I'd already thought about it and I decided that's exactly what happened: I had shot a shadow. Herman Hulce had got between me and the little night light casting a sharp black shadow on the wall outside the bedroom door. I fired and hit the shadow dead center, making a hole in the wall. Hulce, not expecting to be shot at, then fled the scene.

"Look, Ronnie, there's bound to be footprints in the yard. I know who it was. The guy's name is Herman…" I said but I was interrupted by Ronnie.

"Let's go look for the tracks." Ronnie was taking out his flashlight and we went back outside and walked around the yard outside the back door, but the ground had been well-trampled with lawmen by that time and we didn't find any tracks in the rest of the yard nor the woods. Deputy Ronnie Branch was telling me that I ought to just calm down and go back to bed. Also, he suggested that I unload the gun and put it away before I hurt somebody.

As Ronnie and I argued in the yard a state police cruiser pulled into the yard with the blue lights flashing. Out stepped my old friend E. G. Trasker. He walked over to me and said, "Can we speak for a moment?" I noticed that he looked refreshed for 3 o'clock in the morning. His uniform was immaculate, and the creases were sharp. His hat was squarely placed on his head.

"There is something really wrong here" he began in a low, serious voice once we were away from Ronnie. His hands were on his highly polished gun belt. "The Patrick County Sheriff was on the radio just now instructing his officers to carefully examine the house for any controlled substances. That's not the usual procedure when we have an armed home invasion with shots fired in the middle of the night. What did he just tell you?" Trasker motioned with his head toward Ronnie Branch.

"He said I was shooting at shadows and I should go back to bed and unload my gun and put it away." I answered.

Trasker looked around and then continued. "I advise you to get out of here immediately. Do not stay in this house. Go somewhere safe, preferably far away. As for the weapon, I would keep it loaded and on me constantly. You need to flee Patrick County and never return, and you need to go right now. The law can't or won't protect you and your family here. I can't protect you either. Whatever is going on it's coming from high up. Good luck, sir." And he shook my hand. Trasker called to Ronnie that he didn't think he was needed. He got back into his cruiser, turned off the blue lights and drove away.

I didn't have to pass on Trasker's advice to Nedra. She was throwing clothes and bags into the trunk of her Beemer. "If I forgot something, just take it over to my Momma's." She talked as she worked. "I love you. It's been fun but I didn't sign up for this."

I helped her load her things into the car and in minutes we were done. Nedra strapped Dru into the front seat and kissed me. "Don't try to find us. I might try to contact you later…Good luck, Doc, and take care of yourself. I love you." And she was gone. It would be years before I saw her again.

I went back into my house. All the lights were on and two deputies, Ed Wolfe and Frank Hunter were in the hall, digging away at the bullet hole in the wall with large pocket- knives. "What are you guys doing?" I asked.

"Oh, hey Doc. We're looking for the bullet." Ed Wolfe replied, while Ol' Frank kept digging on my wall. The neat little half inch hole the bullet made was now big enough for a man's fist and I was more than a little aggravated.

"What do you need the bullet for? I fired the gun. The only bullets in the walls are mine and y'all are messin' up my house."

"It's evidence." said Frank as he worked away.

"Evidence of what? I told y'all the son of a bitch never fired his gun and besides, it was a machine gun of some kind so there'd be a whole bunch of holes for y'all to dig in." The hole in my wall was growing bigger by the minute. "It's just as well that he didn't shoot that thing. By the time you guys find a bunch of machine gun bullets I might not have any house left."

Ed Wolfe stopped digging and looked at me. "Doc, the Sheriff said we have to charge you with discharging a firearm in an occupied dwelling…"

"What! Some asshole come sneakin' through my house at 3 in the morning with a machine gun and you're charging me? You're damn straight I'm goin' to discharge my firearm! Wouldn't you?"

"Now just calm down, Doc. It ain't up to us. We're just followin' orders. It's the law."

Vietnam to fall. To a man, they were certain that we would mount a massive rescue mission to go back and finish the thing with a proper victory. My fellow draftees and I would be the bulk of this prospective force. We were being trained for Phase II of the Vietnam Conflict, and we were being trained hard. We studied all the small arms in the inventory and some of the crew-served weapons. We learned about helicopters, close air support and artillery strikes. Some of us went to jump school, some to Ranger school and some of us were selected for a three- week course in intensive hand-to-hand combat. The instructor was Master Sergeant Jackson.

Jackson's father had been a member of the Merchant Marine during World War II. After the war, he took a job with a commercial shipper and was assigned to supervise ship-loading in Durban, South Africa, a seemingly natural assignment for a black man in 1946. He met and married a Zulu woman and brought her back with him to a new job at Dundalk Marine Terminal in New Jersey. They had several children. Future Master Sergeant Jackson was the oldest. The boy always had an interest in athletics, but his small stature made it difficult. Still he did remarkably well in high school football. What he lacked in size, he made up for in speed, strength and ferocity. His coach thought he was one of the quickest most coordinated players he ever coached. The week after graduation, Jackson enlisted in the U. S. Army. It was 1965. The Vietnam War was in full swing.

At first, Jackson was straight leg infantry, going on patrols. He did very well. He had ample courage and was more than willing to engage the enemy, but there was a better job for him. In Vietnam, the Viet Cong used an extensive network of well-built tunnels. When our troops couldn't find the enemy, the enemy was literally under foot, hiding in a subterranean maze, waiting for an opportunity to pop out of a hole, inflict casualties on the Americans and then disappear back underground. At five feet six, Jackson was well-suited to be a tunnel rat. He became one of the brave men who volunteered to go into the tunnels armed with a flashlight, a pistol and a bayonet or knife. The tunnels were extremely dangerous, they were small and often contained booby traps ranging from venomous snakes and explosives to poison gas. When the Viet Cong were encountered underground, the fighting was sudden, desperate and savage. Casualties among the tunnel rats were high in this particularly terrifying war. Jackson became one of the best. He was among the most highly decorated tunnel rats in the war and one of the very few black soldiers in the group.

There was a blemish or two on his record. There were rumors that Jackson enjoyed his job too much, and during his third tour in Vietnam (so the rumors went) he began to kill civilians and even ARVN soldiers whom he thought looked like the VC. Rather than charge him and risk the attendant bad publicity, the Army sent him home where he was hailed as a hero and assigned to teach young Americans the awful work of killing.

So, I found myself seated on green bleachers in the late summer heat of Ft. Bragg, North Carolina listening to a short, very black, very impressive Master Sergeant Jackson. He wore highly polished boots, a brown T-shirt, and fatigue pants. He wore no head gear. He stood in the middle of a large sand pit. There was no sound system to magnify his voice. He didn't need it. His staccato-cadenced speech was clearly heard by each of we forty or so students. His skin glistened with sweat and he was the scariest man I'd ever seen up to that point in my young life.

"Some of you may think that hand-to-hand combat is based on these" and he slapped his hands, his arms and his legs, "but to win it has to also come from here," he touched the side of his head, "and here," he touched his chest over his heart. "You must know what to do and you must have the heart to kill. You have to have the spirit, to overcome your opponent and kill him. None of you have that now. Our society trains you not to kill. My job is to retrain and teach you, teach each of you how to strike another human being and take his life. How to hit with whatever weapon you may have at hand and strike until your opponent is either dead or trying very hard to die."

Each day for three weeks, the Master Sergeant would demonstrate a move on some hapless student then we would pair up and practice on each other. By the end of the day in that hot sand pit we were bruised and sore. You could pick out the members of our class around post. We limped. It was called "hand-to-hand combat" but he taught us how best to kill at close range with pistols or rifles, how to take weapons away from our opponents, he taught us how to slash throats and how to find and slash through the abdominal aorta leading to instant death by exsanguination.

He taught us how to kill with entrenching tools, tent posts, bayonets and clubs of various kinds including rocks, sticks and metal pipes.

"This right here" he said as he held a metal pipe in his right hand and tapped it on his left palm "is a hell of a good weapon. You can hit hard on the top of his shoulders breaking his collar bones. That leaves him defenseless. You can break his legs. You can take his breath away by hitting him in the chest, but to kill him, you have to, hit him in the head. You have to, hit him in the head…hard…over and over. Don't you stop until you smash that head like a melon. Don't you stop 'til you see his God Damned brains! Don't you stop until he is dead or trying very hard to die!" They were words to live or die by.

Jackson even gave us a history lesson. "I'm sure all of you have heard of Custer's last stand where a few hundred Indians wiped out a couple of hundred soldiers in what was basically a gun fight. Three years after that little disaster, on January 22, 1879, at a place called iSandlwana, my ancestors, the Zulu wiped out a force of British soldiers numbering just under two-thousand men. They killed them all, and for the most part they killed them with spears, short spears. As the Zulu hit an enemy, they called out the war-cry 'uSuthu'. It gave them courage and strength. Say it! uSuthu! Say it again! Use it. When it comes time for you to kill a man so close that you hear his breath, you smell his body and you feel his blood and brains, you say that! uSuthu! uSuthu! uSuthu! We were all on our feet. Leaping in the air and shouting the Zulu war cry in a frenzied passion. uSuthu! uSuthu! uSuthu! As I looked around at the expressions on the faces of my classmates it came to me. I understood. The idea wasn't to "overcome the training of society" but to overcome sanity itself. It has been thus for as long as men have killed each other. Before you can kill, you must first become crazy. uSuthu! uSuthu! uSuthu! We were driven to the same high pitch of insanity that consumed a long ago Zulu impi before it attacked the British at iSandlwana killing every one of the enemy, then driving them out of their land.

Sometime after the class was over, I ran into Master Sergeant Jackson. "You'll do all right, Boy. You're a murderous little son of a bitch." It was a high compliment; but I'd been accepted into veterinary school and how murderous would an Army veterinarian have to be?

I decided not to wait for Hulce to come to me. I would have to go to him. If I waited on him to make the first move, he could pick the time and place. He could create the situation to his advantage. He could follow Nedra and Druisilla. I had to get him before that happened. I remembered that Randy McAllen, the grizzled biker in my office had mentioned the Double Duce in Danville, so I went there and started watching the place every night from the shadows along the edge of the shopping center parking lot. I turned the tables on Hulce. Now I was the predator. I was the hunter and I would give him as little chance to save himself as I could.

He was there. The big shiny white Caddy would pull in about 9 o'clock each night. Herman would go into the bar and stay until closing time, usually well after midnight. He was always one of the last to leave the place, but I wanted no witnesses at all. No one who might interfere. No one who might try to save Herman Hulce from me. As I watched him from the deep shadows, I felt my anger and my hatred grow. My stomach would be in a knot as I prepared to make my move only to have another late patron come out of the bar.

Then came the chance I'd been waiting for. The big white car was all alone in the middle of the parking lot illuminated by the yellow glow of the parking lot lights. Hulce came out of the Double Duce. He was staggering. Good. He was drunk. Another advantage for me. I would need it. He was bigger and obviously stronger than me. I assumed, he carried a gun at all times. In any kind of fair fight, he could beat me man-to-man and take the pipe right out of my hands and beat me with it. He could also pull out a gun and shoot me dead. My own death didn't worry me, it was that Hulce might save himself. He could survive. I was terrified; terrified of failure. I had to succeed. I had to kill this son of a bitch Herman Hulce.

I was wearing black track shoes, black sweatpants, a black sweat shirt, black leather gloves and a black watch cap. Even though the night was cool, I was hot and sweating.

When Herman reached the big white Cadillac, he staggered a bit and leaned back against the left rear door as he fumbled with his keys. I moved along the shadows on the edge of the parking lot so that I could approach him from behind. I started my run toward him. In the yellow-orange light the black clothes made little difference. I was easily visible if someone looked at me. I was scared for a minute that he would turn around and just shoot me while I was running toward him. I also thought he might get into his car and drive away leaving me standing in a vacant parking lot feeling like a damn fool. But instead he lit a cigarette. Smoking and drinking can in fact be hazardous to your health.

I was running flat out over the last yards. In my head I heard the words: "Hit him in the head! Hit him hard over and over! Don't stop until he is dead or trying very hard to die! Until he is dead or trying very hard to die! Until he is dead or trying very hard to die!"

I practically flew around the trunk of the big white car and with the pipe high in my right hand I hit Herman Hulce on the left side of his head. He looked at me. No expression on his face. After the first blow he turned his body slightly toward me, but it was too late. He was almost half a foot taller than me, but I was jumping up and raining blows onto the top of his nearly bald white head. He began to slide down against the side of the car, slumping down to my height. I grabbed the pipe in both hands now and began to deliver powerful over-hand blows on his skull. I wielded the pipe as if I were chopping wood with an axe. In the bright yellow light, I could clearly see his dead eyes and expressionless face as he continued to slide down into a sitting position on the ground with his back against the rear door of the shiny white car now splattered with blood. I was in a rage. I was driving home each blow with violent force. "Until he is dead or trying very hard to die! Until you see his God Damned brains!"

My blows were slowing. I was tiring. I had never been so tired. My strength was nearly spent. Each blow now brought large splashes of blood and I could see that I was deforming his skull. Hulce was fully seated on the ground now. His long legs straight out in front of him. He was still breathing but noisily. Blood was coming from his nose, mouth and ears. He raised his right arm up toward me, either in a feeble attempt to defend himself or as a plea for mercy. "This one is for Michelle Frazier you bastard!" I panted as I delivered one last terrible crashing blow. "uSuthu!" I cried. His skull split like a melon. I could see his God Damned brains. His right arm dropped. It was over. Herman Frederick Hulce was dead. I don't know if he heard or understood anything I said in the last split seconds of his life, but it is pleasant to imagine that as that son of a bitch fell down that long drop into the deepest pits of Hell, he knew that justice had been done for Michelle Frazier and ringing in his racist ears was a Zulu war cry.

Exhausted I stared at the essentially headless seated corpse. I could not have raised the pipe another time. I myself was defenseless. I couldn't have run. If another person had come up, I wouldn't have run away nor fought, but no one came. As I watched, the hideous thing that had once been Herman Hulce slowly fell onto its right side leaving a smear of blood on the shiny white door of the Cadillac. In my best imitation of Andy Pense with his British accent I said out loud, "Fuck 'em if they can't take a joke."

I noticed that Hulce had been well-armed. He wore two large automatic pistols in shoulder holsters and the MP-40 was clearly visible on the back seat of the car. Lucky for me, he never got a chance to fight back. I was beginning to catch my breath; I pulled off my watch cap and shook my sweat-soaked hair. I then walked slowly across the large empty parking lot to my jeep. As I looked in the rearview mirror, I was amazed at the amount of blood on my face. I smiled and the smile became laughter. Had I gone insane? Was I finally crazy? Probably.

I pulled into a funeral home overlooking highway 58 and disposed of my black blood-covered clothes into a dumpster and wiped my face. I watched the highway for speeding police cars with their blue lights flashing or even an ambulance, but there was nothing. At dawn I pulled out onto 58 and headed back to Patrick County. I stopped at the Spoon Creek Bridge and threw the blood-caked pipe into the stream. Then I went on to work. Just another day.

The mess that was Herman Hulce was discovered around 6:30 a.m. by the workers who cleaned up the parking lot. At first, the Danville Life Saving Crew was called but it was obvious that there was no life to be saved, so the Pittsylvania Coroner arrived. A sheet was draped over the remains and the area was outlined with yellow crime-scene tape. Eventually two patrol officers and two major crime detectives arrived. Gingerly, they removed the wallet.

One of the detectives was Mike Graham. Mike had begun his career as a road deputy in Stokes County and was the first officer on the scene of the Michelle Frazier assault. He instantly recognized the name Herman Hulce. The case had bothered him for years. He and all the other Stokes County officers believed that Hulce had gotten away with something worse than murder.

ain't it? So, Judgie Wudgie, I'm goin' to take real good care of you so you'll live as long as you can and suffer as much as the Good Lord will let you."

That same afternoon in Collinsville, Virginia, just north of Martinsville, there was a violent head on collision on business 220. A small station wagon was knocked onto its right side. The driver scrambled out the window just as orange flames appeared in the front wheel wells. The driver was a mother and her two children, a four-year-old and a two-year-old were strapped into car seats in the back seat. The mother was hysterical.

As fate would have it, Paul Campbell, my EMT instructor was just exiting a nearby restaurant. Paul took in the scene in seconds and sprinted to the car, leaping up onto the wreck and pulling open the left rear door. He dropped inside and used his pocketknife to slice through restraining belts. The entire car was now covered in a cloud of thick black smoke. With a screaming precious child under each arm, Paul pulled himself from the wreckage and ran for life itself. Behind him the car exploded into a huge fireball.

Also, as fate would have it, there was a film crew doing an advertisement for a nearby car dealership. The director moved his crew into the street and caught the entire event on high quality video tape. That night, the tape played on all the national news casts. Within the next five days it played on most local TV news casts. A still photo of Paul and the children with the exploding car in the background was on the front page of papers all over the world.

A perky local newswoman talked Paul into an interview. "What's it feel like to save a life like that?"

Paul looked a bit astonished at such a stupid question, but he had a way with words.

"Why, it's almost like being in love."

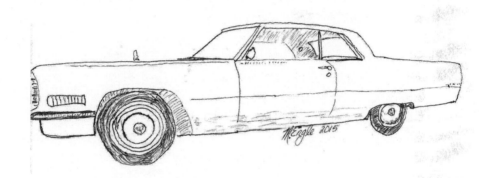

CHAPTER THIRTEEN

2016

Patrick County hasn't changed much. It's still one of the most beautiful places on earth. There are fewer people living here. The birth rate has gone down, retirees are moving into the County to take advantage of the natural beauty. The aging population means that deaths exceed births. U. S. Highway 58 is now four lanes from the Henry County line to the foot of the mountain. There are also four stoplights! Primland is one of the top-rated resorts in the world and has a nationally ranked golf course. We're promoting tourism, so, as they say, come see us. You can have your picture taken on the Spoon Creek Bridge, although today it's a new bridge and not the same one as in my story.

The JEB Stuart Volunteer Rescue Squad is better than ever with large numbers of volunteers. The practice of soft-billing solved most of the financial problems and the squad recently doubled the size of their crew-hall. Big, modern well-equipped ambulances are used which in no way resemble the old van-type ambulances I rode in.

The hospital is now operated by a large corporation that specializes in the management of small rural critical-care-designated facilities. Today there is much more oversight and technological advances making fraud and financial irregularities less likely to occur.

A medevac helicopter is quartered full time at Blue Ridge Airport a few miles away in Henry County so when needed the modern purpose-built helicopter responds within minutes from there instead of from Winston-Salem.

Four-lane highways, stricter drunk driving laws and aggressive law enforcement along with safer cars and airbags have dramatically reduced the number of deaths and serious injuries associated with automobile accidents. An aging population and an influx of retirees from other areas has shifted the major roll of rescue squads from removing victims from wreckage to transporting the elderly sick.

I quit running calls shortly after the death of Herman Hulce. With new recruits the squad really didn't need my services anymore. Now as I ride around the County, I am haunted by the ghosts of the hundreds of calls I ran. There are certain curves in the road, certain stretches of narrow two- lane black top and certain buildings, fields and even trees where the dramatic business of saving lives was carried out. These are the battlefields in the war against injury, disease and death itself. As with all battlefields, they are hallowed places of somber reverence and the memories of long-ago strife.

Nedra LaPeltier fled that terrible night from Patrick County to Myrtle Beach, South Carolina where she was welcomed and sheltered by her father's family. In time, she resumed her nursing career at the Conway, South Carolina hospital, the same hospital where a long-ago nurse inspired Nedra to join the nursing profession. Later, Nedra accepted a better career offer with a large hospital in Charleston, South Carolina. She met a handsome young investment banker who was recovering from multiple fractures incurred in a hang-gliding mishap. They were soon married. The new family moved to Knoxville, Tennessee and eventually to Atlanta where Nedra's husband became an important executive in C & S Bank. Nedra has appeared as a guest on a few episodes of *The Real Housewives of Atlanta*. Druisilla, her daughter became a CPA and married a client who owned a pesticide business. I still see Nedra from time to time, mostly at the funerals of our mutual friends or holidays when she comes home to visit her mother. We're still friends and we talk from time to time. She read this novel before publication and told me I would probably be sued, shot or arrested!

Anthony Price died in 2005 at the age of 81 from complications of diabetes. Anthony had touched many lives in the county and his funeral was one of the biggest in memory. He had been a school bus driver for almost twenty years and a JEB Stuart ambulance driver for nearly that long. A Patrick County School bus was used as the hearse. Most of us who served on the rescue squad with Anthony attended including his nephew Jarrell.

Jarrell Price messed around for several years, dating many different girls, dropping out of school and bouncing around between several dead-end jobs. Then one day he got his act together, went back to Patrick Henry Community College, then to Radford College and after two tries he was accepted into the Medical College of Virginia where he distinguished himself as a top student. After an internship and residency, he eventually became head of emergency services at the Martinsville hospital. He serves as medical director for the local rescue squads and is well-known for volunteering his time to work with squad members. Jarrell married a high school classmate and they have four children.

C. Charles Moran, known as "C. C." my attorney in Stuart was true to his word. He lived less than a year after my visit to his office: not nearly long enough to get me out of legal hot water. He took his own advice on how to handle a personal crisis: take some time off and go to the beach. After his physician in Winston-Salem told him that he had tumors in his lungs and liver, he went to Myrtle Beach and it was there that he suffered a fatal heart attack while watching a magnificent sunrise from the balcony of his luxurious hotel room. I miss him. Of all the lawyers I have come in contact with, C. C. was always honest with me and conducted himself honorably. I suspect he knew as well or better than anyone about the then corruption in Patrick County, but I also suspect he realized that open opposition on his part would be pointless and self-destructive. Sometimes I wish I had felt the same way.

The Judge lived nearly a fifth of his long life encased in a body that would not respond to his commands. He was almost a hundred years old when he inhaled his last breath alone in a private room at the Russell Nursing Home. John Powers had kept him alive as long as he could, but the frailties of age prevented John from keeping the old Judge in his own home. So, the last six months of the Judge's very long life were spent in the nursing home. During that entire six months, not one visitor came to see him. After his death, the County began naming streets and public buildings after him. A monument was erected to his memory. Sometimes if I'm out late at night and no one is around to watch, I make a point of stopping to urinate on this memorial.

John Powers is quite elderly and in his own words, "Don't get out much anymore." Arthritis has made walking very difficult and has bent his spine. He suffers from retinal degeneration his eyesight is nearly gone. He did live to see the death of the Judge and to duly collect his rather large inheritance. A good portion of his inherited wealth went to establish a fund to assist young people with educational expenses or to set up their own business. John does get a number of visitors and I am one. John Powers may have an old body, but his mind is as sharp as ever. He helped quite a bit by providing vital information for this book.

all of us by transferring to UNC/Charlotte where he graduated after two years. He met a pre-dental student at UNC-C and married her. Dairy Queen worked with Larry providing him with managerial jobs throughout their system. Eventually, he earned an MBA from Duke and is now a Vice President with Dairy Queen living in Charlotte with his wife, a dentist, and their two children. That's a long way from Lucille Cane's basement!

Dr. Francis Richter was washed up in Patrick County after the Linda Faye Fretwell case. Accordingly, he resigned his position and signed on with a small rural hospital in central North Carolina. Within a year he was sued for medical malpractice and his medical license was revoked by the North Carolina Medical Board. This time, rather than allowing him to resign, the hospital fired him. In effect, his medical career was over. He spent a couple of miserable years as a drug company representative calling at doctor's offices before attending cooking classes and becoming a chef. He is now an assistant chef at a large resort in upstate New York. He is both successful and happy. It just goes to show that you have to find your niche.

Sheriff Frank Watson was arrested in a public bathroom with a male prostitute in Greensboro, North Carolina. His defense was that he was doing "research." He was convicted of misdemeanor public lewdness and immediately resigned as Patrick County Sheriff. So much for the dynasty of Sheriff Doyle Watson. Just as well. The new Sheriff is named Richard Prescott and he seems to be quite honest and dedicated to doing a good job.

E. G. Trasker is now a senior sergeant in the Virginia State Police in Salem. He is eligible for retirement, but he wants to work as long as he can. He sees to it that the State Police dogs in our area come to me for routine care and I never charge for that service. I rarely see him, but when I do, he is as formal and humorless as he ever was. Although, he does nearly smile from time to time.

I never knew what Lucinda Gray was doing when she wasn't running calls. It turns out she was taking classes at Patrick Henry and Averette eventually graduating with a degree in education. She became an English teacher at South Stokes High School. We were all surprised. I wasn't so surprised when she became involved with Earl Ashe. Earle went back to Virginia Tech and now teaches Science at South Stokes. They never got married, probably a nod to their rebellious youth, but they do live together in a very nice home near Germanton. Earl and Lucinda don't look like they did in their younger days. In fact, they appear more or less like a couple of conventional school- teachers.

Mary Dell Oates continues her old job in Roanoke. She worries that someone may appear in a prosecutor's office to have a soul-cleansing confessional. I worry about that myself. After all, she's not the only one who could be charged with a felony in that case.

On a hot summer afternoon not long ago, I was returning to my clinic after pulling a calf. I had my windows rolled down and was traveling on four-lane US Highway 58. I became aware of a particularly loud motorcycle pulling up beside me. At first, I didn't pay much attention, but it became apparent that the motorcycle was pacing me. I looked over and was startled to see that the rider was an old man with long flowing white hair and a beard. He was riding without a helmet. The motorcycle was a huge customized Harley-Davidson. He squinted at me with his scary eyes. I may have imagined it, but I think he lifted his chin, an imperceptible lift perhaps. A sign of recognition? A gesture of shared memories from long ago? Who knows? Then he hit the throttle and roared away leaving me as if I were standing still. On the back of his blue jean cut-offs was a large patch. A Pagan's patch.

Walter Mayhew is fatter, uglier, older and more obnoxious. In other words, he is the same as he was years ago! All he does is brag about all the lives he saved back in our rescue squad days. Since he developed several skin cancers, he no longer vacations at Myrtle Beach. Now he goes to Cherokee, North Carolina where he hangs out in the casino bragging about what a big shot he is back home.

Rusty Wilcox the red-headed enthusiastic kid, became a paramedic and went to work in Baltimore eventually becoming Chief of the Baltimore City EMS. The job has a lot of headaches, but it pays well. He needs a big paycheck. He married a beautiful Catholic woman from Baltimore, and they have six children. When he gives speeches to the local clubs and groups around Baltimore, he usually tells a story or two about running calls with a small rural volunteer rescue squad in Southside Virginia named after our Confederate General.

Ed Quinn died of a sudden cardiac event in 2008. I suppose the years with a steady diet of bacon, scrambled eggs and Coca Cola finally caught up with him. The funeral brought all the surviving members of JEB Stuart

Volunteer Rescue Squad from those days together again. Maggie Engel showed up and so did Nedra. A large number of radios and beepers were handed out to the mourners. As the casket was lowered into the ground, Patrick County dispatch set off the attention tones. All of the beepers and radios in the crowd responded so the transmission was easily heard. The dispatcher requested a response from Ed's old rescue squad number. Of course, there was no response. This was repeated three times. Finally, the dispatcher said, "Rest well Ed Quinn. Job well done." This is a ceremony referred to as "the last call," and on that fine spring day in the cemetery I thought back to the calls that Ed and I had run and all our shared experiences. I considered my own mortality, my own frailty, and that one by one we were all dying: the people who had been so important in my life. I was embarrassed to find that I was weeping. As I wiped my eyes, I looked around and noticed that all the mourners were crying as well.

As we walked back to our cars, wiping our eyes, hugging each other and saying goodbyes that might be final, suddenly the air was filled with the loud strains of Manfred Mann's Earth Band performing *Quinn the Eskimo*. Larry Cane had a monstrous sound system in the back of his SUV. Now we were all laughing and crying and soon we were all singing along.

> *When Quinn the Eskimo gets here,*
> *Everybody's gonna jump for joy*
> *Come on without, Come on Within.*
> *You'll not see nothing like the Mighty Quinn…*

Carolyn Miller has scarcely aged over the last twenty-five years. Maybe it's that her disheveled appearance made her look twenty-five years older back then. She still runs an occasional rescue squad call, although she tries to pick quiet non-emergency transports. She has held almost every position you can hold in the squad. If you strike up a conversation with her, it won't be long before she starts showing you pictures of her numerous grandchildren. She keeps in constant touch with Maggie Engle on Facebook.

Rosalind considered moving back to England or to Australia. She has relatives in both countries, but after long consideration, she decided that she has more friends in Patrick County so she has stayed here with the bookstore. She ran for the local school board and has been elected and re-elected several times. She is an elder at the Presbyterian Church and a member of the Library Board of Trustees. She is a very active member of our theater group and while she rarely takes a part herself, she delights in directing the plays and in molding actors from shy locals. The plays are excellent, and I never miss one.

Rosalind is as beautiful as ever. If anything, the years have made her more so. I spend as much time as I can with her talking about a wide range of subjects. Andy's name inevitably comes up. She told me that she thinks of him constantly. Staying in Patrick County in the bookstore makes her feel closer to him. A lot of the background information for this book came from Rosalind during our long afternoon discussions over tea. Talking with Rosalind, I realize that I really didn't know what was going on back in those days.

One day I received a huge wooden box sent by an attorney in Washington, D.C. Taped to the crate was a letter from the lawyer informing me that this was my inheritance from Andy. I opened the box to find a priceless original bronze statue by Frederick Remington titled *The Rattlesnake*. It portrays an unfortunate cowboy on a bucking horse with a rattlesnake on the ground below. There was a hand-written note from Andy. "This reminds me of you: Cowboy, Horse, Snake, the Gambino Family. You see, it was a gift to me from Carlo Gambino for spring cleaning. Cheers, Andy."

Over the years, many of us wondered why the Gambino's hadn't bumped us off in Patrick County, we who had damaged their money-laundering scheme. Maybe Andy had something to do with it. Why did the head of the Gambino Family give Andy such a valuable gift anyway? I asked Rosalind and she said, "Andy's forte was keeping secrets and sadly he took most of them to his grave. I always thought he should have written a book."

I always thought that she should have written a book. Maybe several books.

As for me, well, hell. I never could keep a secret.

The Rattlesnake by Frederick Remington